THE CASE OF THE MISSING PUFFINS

A Cousins' Caper Mystery

Kate Meadows

STONE PATH
PUBLISHING

Stone Path Publishing LLC

ISBN-13: 979-8-218-90529-3

First Edition 2026..

To my husband and best friend, Pete, thank you for believing in my dreams, even when they were only just taking shape, and for always standing beside me with love and encouragement. To Jake, Allie, Luke, Cody, and Olivia, may this story carry you back to family adventures in Maine, to salty air, laughter, and the memories we've made together over the years. And to Amelia, Jake, and Henry, this book is for you, and for all the Maine adventures still awaiting us. I can't wait to share this story with you and to create many more together.

contents

Chapter 1 – Welcome to Bar Harbor

Luke pressed his forehead against the train window, watching as the coastline appeared in the distance. Rocky cliffs giving way to deep blue water, waves pounding the rocks, and pine trees ascending like green towers into the cloudless royal blue sky.

Alex gave a nod, a feeling of anticipation building in him as they neared the town. "It's like we leave the rest of the world behind when we get to Bar Harbor with no school, no schedules; just Grandma, the house, and the whole Maine wilderness."

The train gave a long, low whistle as it began to slow, the sound echoing across the rocky shore. As the doors opened, a rush of air carried in the fragrance of saltwater, spruce, and distant bonfires. They got off the train, their backpacks bouncing and sneakers hitting the platform, as if they had arrived home.

Grandma Maggie stood waiting just past the fence next to her shiny black SUV, wearing her favorite floppy sunhat. She waved both hands as if they were returning heroes. Perched proudly in the front seat, Bear, their grandmother's massive Maine Coon cat, winked languidly at them, his tufted ears twitching.

"There you are!" Grandma called out, her voice comforting and familiar. "Took you long enough! I've been standing here for ten whole minutes. I almost grew roots!"

Luke laughed and ran ahead, arms open. "We brought our appetites!"

Alex let out a laugh as he caught up. "I brought bug spray so those mutant mosquitoes can't turn me into an all-you-can-eat buffet again this summer!"

Grandma pulled them into a hug that carried the scent of lavender and sea air. "You boys get taller every time I see you. I think I will need a few extra boxes of pancake mix this summer."

Luke and Alex had always looked forward to their time in Bar Harbor. They spent part of their summer with Grandma Maggie every year, but this time was different. This time, they were here for the whole summer. No parents, no schedules, no school—just them, Grandma, Bear, and all the adventures they could handle out in the Maine wilderness.

They climbed into the back seat. Bear stretched himself across Luke's lap with an exaggerated sigh, already claiming his favorite spot.

Luke grinned, gently scratching Bear under his chin and kissing him on the head.

Alex let out a laugh, looking out the window as the familiar scenery unfolded. "Bear, you are one of a kind," he said.

Luke leaned back in his seat, gazing out the window as Grandma eased the car away from the train station and down the winding road. They passed spruce trees, cozy cottages, and the sparkling edge of the harbor. And then, there it was, the old wooden Bar Harbor sign, like an old friend welcoming them home. Everything looked just like he remembered.

The water was calm, fishing boats rocking softly on the waves like they were waving hello, while seagulls glided through the fresh air, calling out as if they had a secret to share. The streets were alive with people, tourists, and locals soaking up the sunshine. The cozy, full-of-character shops and restaurants looked like something out of a postcard. It was exactly how Luke had remembered it. He could already feel that special Bar Harbor energy: slow, easy, and full of possibilities. "This place never changes," he spoke quietly, a smile rounding the corners of his lips.

Grandma Maggie glanced at him and nodded. "That's the beauty of it," she said, the kindness in her voice matching the golden rays of sunlight shining through the windows.

Luke leaned forward in his seat; his eyes open wide in excitement. "I love it here." He inhaled deeply. "The blues are bluer, and the greens are greener."

"Hey," Alex said, nudging Luke. "Remember that time we got caught in that storm?"

Luke laughed, glancing at Alex and remembering that day. The first rumble of thunder crashed across the ridge with a warning growl. Luke glanced up from the trail map, gazing intently at the dark clouds climbing over the mountain peaks. "Uh, guys?" he called. "That doesn't look friendly."

Jake, his older brother, shaded his eyes with one hand and let out a low whistle. "Nope, that's a storm front, and it's moving fast. We'd better find shelter before it hits."

Alex, Luke's cousin, partner-in-adventure, and best friend since birth, readjusted his pack straps with a grin. "Race you to find a shelter spot!"

"Not a race," Jake responded, but he was smiling too.

The three of them broke into a jog along the narrow trail, pine needles crunching beneath their feet and the scent of rainfall heavy in the air. They were miles from the nearest road, deep in the mountains of western Maine. The sort of place where cell signals vanished, and you had to rely on your wits, your compass, and your teamwork.

"Let's use that rock ledge up ahead!" Luke shouted, spotting a cluster of boulders jutting from the hillside like a giant's shoulder.

Jake gave an approving nod. "Good eyes! That'll block the wind from the west."

They hurried beneath the ledge as the first drops began to fall. Big, cold splats that quickly turned into sheets of rain. The world went gray and wild, thunder booming overhead.

"Okay, team," Jake remarked, his voice composed even as the storm roared. "What's first?"

Luke pulled off his pack, pulled out his tarp, and spread it out. "Shelter."

Alex was quickly surveying the forest floor for available materials. He crouched low, eyeing a handful of branches at the base of a thick spruce, where the rain hadn't soaked through yet. "I'll grab some pine boughs for insulation," he called. He flipped open his utility knife; its handle worn smooth from years of use. Alex began trimming the lower branches off the nearby pine. The blade made a clean snick with each cut, the keen aroma of sap filling the air. He worked quickly but carefully, choosing branches with soft, full needles that would help block wind and trap warmth.

"Perfect," Jake stated, watching him work. "Good choice to use the green ones, they'll shed the water better. Work fast, but don't rush."

The boys worked like clockwork, years of hiking trips and Grandma Maggie's summer lessons kicking in. Luke tied lines between trees using taut-line hitches; hours of practice made his fingers move with experienced precision. They angled the tarp to shed water and built up the sides with the pine branches. The rain slammed overhead, but the shelter held strong.

When the wind began to howl, Luke grabbed the orange bandana from his pack and tied it high on a stick outside the ledge. "Signal flag," he said proudly.

Alex arched an eyebrow. "You think it'll stay up?"

"Only one way to find out." Said Luke.

Jake laughed softly, adjusting his own rain jacket. "That's the kind of thinking I like—resourceful and a little stubborn."

They all ducked back under the shelter as lightning flashed across the valley. The storm felt like it was alive, rising and falling in waves. Inside their small cocoon of dry space, the boys unpacked the camp stove and huddled close while the blue flame spat to life.

"Dinner time," Alex said, tearing open a packet of oatmeal. "Chef Alex, at your service."

Luke let out a long groan. "Not oatmeal again."

Jake shrugged, wearing that lopsided grin of his. "Well, it's either that or cold granola. Your call."

Luke poked at the pot with his spoon. "Fine. Oatmeal wins," he said, as if surrendering.

A warm mix of cinnamon and oats drifted up, combining with the sharp, wet smell of the pines outside. The forest dripped and whispered as the rain fell steadily on the tarp. Despite the storm, the moment felt calm—safe, even.

For a while, they just sat listening to the rain. The forest had gone from untamed to peaceful, the thunder now distant. Mist curled through the trees like smoke.

When the storm at last eased, they crawled out of their shelter. The forest sparkled beneath a silver haze, every branch shimmering with drops of water.

Luke drew in a long breath.

Jake clapped him on the shoulder. "You handled that storm better than half the guys in my wilderness training group."

Alex grinned. "Because Grandma Maggie taught us well."

Jake gave a nod. "Yeah, she'd be proud. And it's good practice, she's expecting you both to be ready for anything this summer."

Luke turned to look at him, curious. "You mean when we go stay with her?"

"Exactly," Jake remarked. "I'll be around some weekends, but I'll be working at the local airport most of the summer. I need to earn money to pay for flight lessons."

Alex's eyes lit up. "That's awesome! You're really doing it?"

Jake laughed softly, brushing rain off his sleeve. "Yep, it's my big adventure. But I wanted to see how ready you two were before I head off for the summer. I wanted to make sure you can handle yourselves out in the wilderness."

Luke pretended to puff out his chest. "Mission accomplished."

Jake let out a laugh. "No doubt. You stayed calm, used your heads, and worked together. That's what counts."

Luke and Alex traded a grin. They'd been hiking together for as long as they could remember. They had grown up building forts, learning knots, testing gear in Grandma's backyard. They didn't just like being outdoors; they lived for it.

Alex kicked at the mud, smiling. "You always say there's no bad weather, Jake."

Luke joined in, grinning. "Yeah, only unprepared hikers with bad equipment."

Jake laughed, shaking his head. "Exactly. And I got that from Grandma Maggie. You know her, she'd hike through a hurricane just to prove a point."

All three burst out laughing, the sound echoing off the wet rocks.

Jake rested against the boulder, watching them with pride. "You know," he said, "storms like that—they show you what you're made of. Most people only like the outdoors when it's easy. But you two stayed calm, stayed smart, and relied on your experience to make it work. That's what real adventure is."

Luke nodded quietly. "I like that. Even the rain part."

Alex grinned. "Especially the rain part. Makes the world feel... alive."

Jake gave a warm smile. "That's exactly why I love it too. The wilderness always has surprises for you."

They remained side by side, looking out at the mist-covered forest, the smell of spruce and soil enveloping them. Somewhere above, the clouds started to break, letting a few streams of sunlight spill through the trees.

Luke watched the light catch on the orange bandana still fluttering in the breeze. "Guess that means Grandma Maggie would pass us."

Jake chuckled. "She'd give you both an A-plus and probably make you pancakes to celebrate."

That made all three of them laugh again, the kind of laugh that felt warm even in the clammy cold of the storm's aftermath.

For a moment, everything was still. The forest, the air, the relationship they shared, it all felt strong and solid, like the ledge they stood underneath.

Jake slung his pack over one shoulder. "Come on, adventurers. Let's head home before the next cloud decides to test us again."

As they hiked down the muddy trail, Luke looked back one last time at where the little shelter they'd built had been—ropes, tarp, and orange bandana safely packed away, it was like they had never been there. He smiled, already visualizing what the summer's adventures in Bar Harbor might bring.

That thunderous day had earned them more than just wet socks and muddy boots. It earned them trust. After that, their parents were confident the boys could handle themselves in the wild. That's why they were here now, on their own, spending the whole summer with Grandma Maggie in Maine.

Luke's mom, Charlotte, was a park ranger and environmental educator. She taught classes on hiking safety, could name every bird by its call, and always had a trick or two up her sleeve for starting a fire without matches. Luke spent his childhood learning to follow animal trails, read trail signs, and be prepared for anything nature throws at him.

Alex's dad, Nate, worked as an engineer on boats and on navigation systems for small aircraft. His garage was like a mini science lab filled with tools, gadgets, maps, and all kinds of weird gear spread out on every surface. Alex had been learning to follow coordinates before he even knew how to ride a bike without training wheels. Nate was the type of person who always had a backup plan, and a backup plan for the backup plan.

The two families lived near each other, just a short drive apart. Luke lived in New Hampshire, and Alex's house was just across the border in Massachusetts. Their houses were close enough for weekend hikes, backyard camping trips, and making obstacle courses with ropes and pulleys. They were cousins, sure. But they were more than that. They were a team. Between their parents and Grandma Maggie, they were raised with a love for adventure and the great outdoors.

Alex tilted forward. "Speaking of Jake… is he going to have any free time to come to Bar Harbor?"

Luke's smile relaxed. "He'll visit sometimes, but he's working almost every day at the airport. He's trying to get his first pilot's license. He's training to fly a Cessna now."

Alex's eyebrows rose up. "That's awesome. Maybe he can take us for a ride."

Luke nodded. "Yeah. When Jake gets into something, he's all in, and learning to fly was right up there with piano playing for him. I'm excited for him… I just miss having him around. It's weird without him."

Alex nudged him lightly. "Yeah. But hey, I bet he'll swing by. And until then, we've got Grandma Maggie, Bear, and miles of wilderness."

Luke smiled. "True."

Grandma Maggie looked back over her shoulder and said, "I've got plenty of trails and chores saved up for you two." They both groaned in unison, which made her laugh.

Luke rolled down the window, feeling the cool breeze rush in as Grandma steered the car up a gravel driveway that gave them a perfect view of the harbor. "You smell that?" he asked, slightly leaning his head out. "Ocean, roses, and something baking."

Grandma grinned, glancing at him. "That's the salt mist roses blooming along the porch. And a fresh blueberry pie cooling on the windowsill. Thought you'd want dessert before dinner." Alex groaned in appreciation, a big grin spreading across his face. "Best summer already." Luke smiled, nodding in agreement. Back home, their friends Jason and Malik were probably glued to the couch, controllers in hand, air conditioning blasting. It sounded nice. But not as nice as this. Not as nice as being here. Because this was Maine. It was Grandma's house. And it was all the freedom they could dream of. But neither of them realized, what neither of them could have known, was that this summer would turn out to be unlike any other. Full of secrets, hidden signals, and a mystery waiting for them on the cliffs beyond the lighthouse.

And Grandma Maggie? Well, she had a few secrets of her own.

Chapter 2 – Brushstrokes and Secrets

Luke and Alex had only been at their grandmother's house in Maine for two whole days, and already it felt like they'd been there forever. Every nook of the house seemed to wink at them—the wooden floors creaked in all the right places as if the house were whispering, *"Welcome back, kids."* The air smelled of pine, lavender, and something delicious baking in the kitchen, and sunlight danced across the handmade patchwork quilts on their beds.

Their room was a tiny universe all its own: shelves crammed with postcards, old trinkets gathered from summers past, and mysterious jars whose contents they swore changed when no one was looking. They could launch epic pillow battles, build forts that touched the ceiling (almost), and laugh so loud that the walls seemed to giggle back.

Here, time moved funny—slow enough to notice the tiniest things, like dust floating like tiny fairies, but fast enough to fill every day with a new adventure. Even the quiet moments felt like magic, as if the house remembered every prank, secret handshake, and whispered story from summers past.

The salt air rolled in from the harbor every morning, carrying the scent of seaweed and roses. Gulls cried from overhead. The breeze rustled the trees along the bluff. Everything about it whispered, "Adventure."

Grandma Maggie's house sat on a gentle rise overlooking Bar Harbor. It had gray shingles, white trim, a wraparound porch with creaky floorboards and Adirondack chairs, and a view that looked like an artist had painted it. Salt mist roses climbed along the railing, their soft pink petals swaying in the breeze. The scent followed you wherever you went.

Grandma Maggie served up her famous breakfast of Dirty Potatoes with eggs, toast, and fruit on her handmade plates. "I started pottery a long time ago," she told them, refilling their orange juice. "Back when your Uncle John and I were working long hours. I needed something that let me slow down and clear my mind. Clay doesn't rush. It listens, teaches you things."

Luke ran his fingers over the edge of his plate. "They're amazing."

"Well," Grandma smiled, "they're sturdy. And that's what counts."

Bear, her enormous Maine Coon cat, dozed in a patch of sun near the porch steps, paws in the air and tail flicking lazily.

"Grandma," Alex laughed, "Why do you call these Dirty Potatoes?"

Grandma Maggie chuckled, "Well, when Jake was little, he thought that the brown bits on the fried potatoes mixed with the browned ground beef made them look dirty. That's what Jake called them, and the name just stuck."

"Well, whatever you call them, they are delicious and my favorite!" Alex replied.

After breakfast, the boys wandered out into the backyard while Grandma headed into town to deliver new pieces of her pottery to a local gallery. They sat on the grass, sipping cold lemonade and talking about the day. That's when Luke looked over at the old pottery studio. It sat behind the garden, with weathered wood, faded trim, and one window partly fogged with years of clay dust and ocean air.

"You know what we should do?" Luke said, sitting up.

Alex raised an eyebrow. "Fix up the shed?"

Luke grinned. "Paint it. Surprise Grandma. It looks like it's been through a dozen nor'easters."

Alex nodded slowly. "We'd have to move fast. She'll be back before dinner."

"I'll grab the paint. You grab the brushes."

They made a beeline for the garage.

The garage was more of a barn, really—wooden beams, a slanted roof, and the faint scent of motor oil and dried grass. The light inside came from one dusty window and a single bulb that flickered to life when Luke flipped the switch. They rummaged through old shelves and found two cans of paint—coastal blue and seafoam green. The labels were curled and cracked, but the paint inside looked usable. They grabbed brushes, rollers, a drop cloth, and sandpaper.

Alex pushed aside some old Christmas decorations and reached into a crate of old gardening tools. His hand brushed something strange, a small wooden box. "What's this?" he said, opening the box. Inside was a heavy brass device, about the length of a flashlight, with more than a dozen rotating disks stacked along its spine, each etched with a full alphabet in uneven, worn letters. A cracked leather strap held the whole thing together like a relic from another era.

It looked more like a strange puzzle than a tool. Luke squinted. "Looks old. Maybe military?"

Alex turned it in his hands. "Think it's Grandma's?"

"Probably. Grandma Maggie keeps everything." Luke shrugged. "We should ask her."

Alex tucked it back where he found it, for now. They were on a mission.

They carried everything out to the shed and got to work. The coastal blue paint went on smoothly, while the seafoam green made the door pop. Luke added a row of tiny seashells around the window frame while Alex touched up the edges with quiet precision.

Bear relocated to a bench nearby, watching them like a sleepy supervisor.

Once Luke and Alex had finished painting, they cleaned up and then focused on the garden beds lining the walkway. A few pots were already there, cracked and half-full of dry soil.

"We should add some flowers," Luke said, brushing his hands off.

Alex pointed to a flat of small starter plants near the fence. "Grandma Maggie must have gotten those at the Farmer's Market in town," Alex said.

"Marigolds, daisies, and... is that lavender?" said Luke.

They filled the old terracotta pots with fresh soil from the compost bin behind the garage. Alex used a hand trowel to loosen the marigolds' roots before planting them. He remembered something he'd learned from a gardening workshop with his mom. "Gotta break up the roots a little so they can spread in the new soil," he explained.

Luke patted the dirt around a daisy. "You're like a flower surgeon."

They gave the plants a deep watering, making sure the soil absorbed it all. "We'll need to check these every morning," Alex said. "They'll dry out fast; the sun hits this side of the shed most of the day."

Just as they finished rinsing the paint off their arms at the hose, the sound of tires crunching on gravel signaled Grandma's return. She stepped out of the SUV, paused, and blinked at the shed. "Oh, my word," she whispered. She walked slowly toward it, her fingers brushing the fresh paint. "You boys did this?"

Luke and Alex stood in the grass, nodding sheepishly.

"It was Luke's idea," Alex said. "We just wanted to surprise you."

Grandma turned to them, eyes glassy with tears, and hugged them both. "You boys," she said softly, "have no idea how much this means to me."

Bear meowed in agreement, stretching out in the grass.

"Well," Grandma said, composing herself, "I suppose this calls for a proper thank-you dinner."

That night, the kitchen filled with the buttery scent of her famous lobster mac and cheese. Luke and Alex set the table, carefully placing more of Grandma's pottery plates out. No two matched, but they all looked like they belonged together. She pulled a strawberry shortcake from the fridge and placed it in the center of the table.

"You know," she said, slicing generous pieces, "tomorrow might be the perfect day for a puffin-watching tour."

Luke's head shot up. "Really?"

Alex leaned forward. "We've never seen puffins up close before."

Grandma winked. "Then it's settled. We'll pack a lunch, grab the binoculars, and catch the morning boat. Just be sure to dress warmly, it can get pretty cold out on the water, even in the summer."

After dinner, as they washed dishes together, Luke glanced out the window toward the studio.

"That old thing in the garage," he said. "We should ask her about it tomorrow."

Alex nodded. "Yeah. I've never seen anything like it."

Outside, the sun dipped into the sea, casting a golden path across the water. Bear curled at the foot of the table, full and content. The boys didn't know it yet, but like the boat ride tomorrow, that brass cylinder was the beginning of something much bigger than they could imagine.

Directions:

1. Cook bacon until golden and crispy. Stove or oven—your choice. Set bacon aside on paper towels. **SAVE THE BACON FAT:**

2. Boil potatoes in salted water until just fork-tender. (12-15 min). Drain and cool. Better if cooked the night before and kept cold.

3. Dice potatoes into small cubes.

4. In another pan, brown the ground beef. Drain all the fat. Set aside.

5. Heat bacon fat in a big skillet. Add potatoes and fry until golden and crispy. Dont rush them.

6. Add ground beef, salt, and pepper.

7. Stir gently.

Serve with... • **Toast & Coffee**

Chapter 3- The Puffin Cruise and the Light Beyond the Fog

The next morning, the kitchen was filled with the warm, buttery aroma of Grandma's special cinnamon-dusted blueberry muffins. Luke and Alex hurried downstairs, drawn in by the smell, and found a breakfast spread waiting for them—muffins, fresh fruit, and a steaming pot of coffee for Grandma.

"You boys better eat up," Grandma said, setting two mismatched, hand-thrown pottery plates on the table. "We've got a boat to catch."

Bear lounged on the windowsill, blinking sleepily at the morning sun.

After breakfast, the boys packed a bag with sunscreen, binoculars, notebooks, and snacks for the ride. Alex, always prepared, had his backpack filled with a first-aid kit, a compass, an extra water bottle, and a poncho, just in case.

The walk down to the harbor took them along Bar Harbor's cobblestone streets, lined with brightly colored shops and hanging flower baskets. Seagulls wheeled overhead as fishing boats bobbed in the water. The salty tang of the ocean mixed with the scent of fried clams drifting from nearby seafood shacks.

The tour boat, a sturdy white vessel named *The Island Spirit*, was waiting at the dock. As they stepped aboard, a woman in a red bandana greeted them.

"Welcome aboard!" she said. "I'm Captain Emily. Today, we're headed out to see some of the most charming seabirds on the East Coast—puffins!"

Luke grinned as he found a spot near the railing. "This is going to be awesome."

Grandma sat beside them, wrapping a shawl around her shoulders. "Your grandfather and I used to take this tour every summer," she said with a smile. "He swore he once saw a puffin wink at him. I told him it was probably just the sun in his eyes."

Alex turned toward her. "Did you really use to go puffin watching?"

"Oh yes," she said. "And not just puffins. We used to track whale migrations, count seals, and watch storms roll in from the sea. But puffins were always my favorite. So serious looking. Like they have important bird business to attend to."

As the boat zipped past the rocky islands and swishy kelp beds, spray sparkled in the sunlight. Gulls wheeled overhead, calling to one another as if they were sharing secrets.

Then a new voice boomed cheerfully above the engine's hum. "Well now, if you look sharp off the port side..."

Everyone turned. Captain Red Malloy stood near the railing, solid and confident, as he belonged on the water. His weathered red hat sat low on his head, and his eyes scanned the horizon with practiced ease.

"There," he said, pointing past the mist. "That's Stormwatch Light."

Luke leaned over the rail. At first, he saw only fog. But then the mist thinned, and a tall, crooked shape appeared on a jagged rock, rising straight out of the waves.

The lighthouse looked tired, as if it had been standing guard for far too long. Its stone walls were chipped and cracked, and the glass in the lantern room was shattered, glittering faintly like broken ice. Ivy climbed up one side, wrapping around the tower in a long green stripe, like a scar from an old adventure.

"Been abandoned for years," Captain Red went on. "My granddad used to tell me that Stormwatch Light never missed a night, until one wild storm came roaring in. Thunder shook the sea, waves climbed higher than houses, and then poof, the light went dark."

Luke imagined the storm: roaring wind, flashing lightning, sailors searching the black water for that guiding glow.

"Some folks say it should've been rebuilt," Red said, scratching his beard. "With new paint. new glass and bright as ever. But others..." He lowered his voice just a little. "Others say it's best left just the way it is."

As they approached the lighthouse, Luke felt a shiver, even though the sun was warm. Stormwatch Light seemed to be watching them back, quiet and almost eerie, as if concealing a secret.

"Sometimes," Red added, sounding almost too casual, "people claim they see lights flashin' up there. Just for a second. Like someone's still tendin' the lamp."

Luke's eyes widened. "But... no one lives there, right?"

Red chuckled. "Not that anyone knows of." He winked. "I chalk it up to reflections. Moonlight. Old ghost stories sailors tell when they've got nothin' else to do."

After the boat passed by, Luke kept looking back. For just a moment, he was sure of it; something glimmered inside the broken lantern room.

Was it a trick of the light? Or was the lighthouse hiding some mystery? Stormwatch Light stood silent behind them, waiting.

Grandma chuckled from her seat. "You boys ever hear the story of the Fogbound Captain?"

Luke turned. "No. Tell us."

"Well," Grandma began, adjusting her shawl with a sly smile, "legend has it, a long time ago, a sea captain and his crew got caught in a terrible storm off Seal Island. The storm came out of nowhere, thick black clouds, lightning cracking across the sky, and the wind howling like a wolf. The sea roared so loud that you could hardly hear the ship's bell. The captain and his crew tried everything possible, but the storm was too powerful. They went down with the ship, swallowed by the sea."

Alex leaned forward, his eyes wide. "That sounds awful..."

Grandma nodded solemnly. "It was. But that's not the end of the story. Locals say that when the mist rises off the water on foggy mornings, and the haze swallows up the cliffs, you can still see his lantern light bobbing just off the coast. It flickers through the fog like it's floating on the water. Some say the captain is still trying to find his way home, searching for the shore and the ship he lost."

Luke shivered, even though the morning sun was warm. "Do people really see it?"

Grandma lowered her voice as though telling them a secret. "Some do, and others... well, they say it's best not to look too closely when the fog rolls in."

Alex raised an eyebrow. "You believe that?"

Grandma gave a knowing smile, her eyes twinkling. "Let's just say I don't walk near the cliffs when the fog rolls in. And if you ever hear the wind howling just right or the sea seems quieter than usual, maybe you'll catch a glimpse of that lantern yourself. But be careful," she warned, her tone turning serious. "If you see it too close, they say the captain will beckon you. And if you follow, you might end up lost like him, forever trying to find your way back to shore."

Alex's heart raced as he looked out at the water. The rising sunlight cast long shadows over the cliffs in the distance. For a moment, the world outside felt strange, as if anything could happen.

"Well," Grandma said, breaking the silence, "we've got an adventure ahead of us, but remember, when you're out there in the wilds, the sea isn't the only thing with secrets."

As the boat slowed, Captain Emily pointed to a rocky island ahead. "Seal Island," she announced. "One of the few places puffins have returned to nest here in Maine."

Passengers gathered at the rail, binoculars in hand. And then, they saw them. Dozens of puffins stood along the rocks like little black-and-white penguins wearing bright orange boots. Their colorful beaks looked like they belonged in a cartoon. Some waddled awkwardly. Others took off and glided just above the water, and a few dove straight into the sea.

"They fly underwater," Alex whispered, amazed.

"They sure do," said a tall woman standing beside them in a tan vest. "I'm Dr. Evelyn Maddox," she said, offering a firm handshake. "I'm a seabird biologist from the local research center. I study puffins, where they nest, how they travel, and what happens when something threatens them. They flap their wings underwater like they're flying through the air. Puffins can dive up to 80 feet deep in search of small fish like herring, sand eels, and capelin."

Luke was glued to his binoculars. "They're incredible."

Dr. Maddox nodded. "They are. And here's something even cooler, puffins have special tongues covered with tiny spines that help them grip fish. They can hold several fish crosswise in their beaks at once and still go after more. Some puffins have been recorded carrying up to ten fish at once!"

"That's wild," Alex said. "Like underwater grocery shopping."

Dr. Maddox laughed. "Exactly. But they need full baskets to survive. And that's getting harder."

"Why?" Luke asked.

"Several reasons," Dr. Maddox said. "Overfishing makes it harder for them to find food. Warmer oceans change where fish live. And predators introduced to islands, like rats or cats, can wipe out entire colonies by eating eggs and chicks."

She paused, her tone thoughtful. "This year's counts are a little lower than expected. We're not sounding alarms yet, but it's something we're watching closely."

Captain Red scratched his chin. "Puffins aren't the only thing that's vanished out here lately. A few local fishermen, myself included, have had gear go missing. Lobster traps, buoys, and even some old lines.

Thought maybe it was storms or strong currents at first, but..." He narrowed his eyes toward Stormwatch Light. "Some of it was in calm waters. Doesn't add up."

Grandma tilted her head. "You think someone's taking it?"

Red shrugged. "Hard to say. But it's enough to make a man look over his shoulder more than usual. Just feels like the sea's keeping more secrets than usual this summer."

Dr. Maddox smiled, like she'd been waiting for this exact moment. "I can tell you boys are curious about nature and the ocean," she said. "And that's a very good thing. In fact, I was just about to invite you to visit our research center."

Luke's eyes grew round as sea glass. "Really?" he asked, hardly able to stay still.

"Really," Dr. Maddox laughed. "You'll get to see how we study sea creatures, test water samples, and protect the coastline. And," she leaned in a little, "we could use your help with something important."

"Tomorrow we're doing a beach cleanup," she continued. "After big storms, the waves leave behind all kinds of surprises—tangled fishing nets, ropes, driftwood, and sometimes even rusty tools from old shipwrecks that have been hiding under the sand for years."

Luke imagined treasure half-buried on the beach, waiting to be discovered.

Grandma lifted an eyebrow and smiled mysteriously. "That's the thing about the ocean," she said. "It has a long memory. You never know what it might give back... or what stories it might be ready to tell."

Luke felt a thrill in his chest. Helping the ocean, and maybe uncovering a secret or two, sounded like the best way to spend a day.

As the boat turned slowly back toward the harbor, the boys kept their eyes on the lighthouse. And just for a moment, as the sun dipped behind a thin band of clouds, Luke saw it—a brief flash of light from the top of Stormwatch Light. Just one. Then gone.

He turned to Alex. "Did you see that?"

Alex shook his head. "What?"

Luke hesitated. "Nothing. Maybe just the sun." But deep down, he wasn't so sure.

Chapter 4 – Trash Bags and Troubling Signs

The next morning dawned bright and breezy, the kind of summer day that made everything sparkle. A pair of herring gulls called from the rooftop as Luke and Alex loaded their backpacks into Grandma Maggie's black SUV. The air smelled like salt and wild roses. Grandma was dressed in hiking boots and a zip-up fleece layered over a bright yellow T-shirt, ready for whatever the day might bring.

"Don't forget to refill your water bottles," she said, handing each one a granola bar. We'll head to the research center first. Dr. Maddox wants to show you her lab."

Luke was practically bouncing in his seat. "I can't wait. Do you think we'll get to see puffins up close?"

"I'm not sure," Grandma said with a smile, "but I bet she's got all kinds of cool things to show you."

Bar Harbor's streets were starting to wake up as they passed through town. Delivery trucks rumbled down alleyways. Store owners hosed off sidewalks. The sea shimmered beyond the trees. The Bar Harbor Wildlife Research Center was located on the edge of town, tucked behind a stretch of spruce forest and overlooking the ocean. It was a long, low building with solar panels on the roof and a wind turbine spinning lazily beside it. A carved wooden sign read, *"Dedicated to the Protection and Study of Coastal Wildlife."* Inside, the lab smelled faintly of brine, fish, and freshly brewed coffee. The entrance opened into a bright lobby with an information board filled with charts, wildlife photos, and tide schedules. There were display cases featuring bird feathers, whale bones, and sculptures made from marine debris, including nets and plastic bottles collected from the shore.

A tall woman in a tan vest appeared from down the hall. "Welcome," Dr. Maddox said, shaking Luke and Alex's hands. "I'm so glad you could visit. I love seeing young people interested in wildlife." She led them down a hallway lined with glass windows, looking into workrooms and labs. The walls were covered with posters of various birds, maps showing migration routes, and pinned feathers. One room held several long tables covered in puffin models, beak samples, and preserved feathers, some displayed under glass cases for study. Another room was filled with microscopes and Petri dishes, where researchers carefully analyzed seawater samples for plankton and pollutants.

"There are many jobs in a place like this," Dr. Maddox explained as they walked. "Some of us are field biologists, like me. We go out into the wild and collect data, count birds, track migration, that sort of thing. Others work in the lab, analyzing the data we bring back. And then we have interns and assistants who help with everything from feeding rescued animals to running software models that predict future migration patterns or breeding success rates."

As they walked past a long counter filled with glowing test tubes and bubbling glass containers, Luke pointed to a researcher pouring seawater into a tray. "What are they looking for?" he asked.

"Looking for microplastics," Dr. Maddox said, pausing beside a wall covered in charts. "They're one of the biggest threats to marine life."

Alex leaned in. "What are microplastics?"

Dr. Maddox smiled. "Great question! Microplastics are teeny-tiny pieces of plastic, smaller than a grain of rice. Some are so small you need a microscope to see them. They come from things like broken plastic bags, old water bottles, or even from clothes made with synthetic fibers. Every time someone washes clothes like fleece or athletic wear, little bits of plastic go down the drain and end up in the ocean."

Luke's eyes widened. "Wait... so the ocean is full of invisible plastic?"

"Unfortunately, yes," she said. "Fish can't tell the difference between microplastics and food, so they eat it. Then bigger fish eat those fish. Eventually, it can even end up in us."

"That's... gross," Alex muttered.

"It is," Dr. Maddox agreed. "But the good news is, there are things we can do."

"Like what?" Luke asked.

"For starters, use less plastic. Choose reusable water bottles, bags, and containers instead of single-use plastic ones. Wear natural fabrics like cotton whenever possible. And always recycle properly. Oh, and if you do beach cleanups like we're doing today, picking up even the smallest piece of trash helps."

"I once found a plastic spoon inside a puffin's nest," she added, walking beside them. "It looked like it had washed up and gotten tangled in the seaweed. That's why what we're doing today matters.

Even one less straw, one less plastic fork, makes a difference. Imagine if every kid did that, how many thousands of pieces of plastic we could keep out of the ocean."

Alex looked at Luke. "I think we should each start a no-plastic challenge at school. Let's see whose school can do the best."

Luke grinned, "Challenge accepted!" And they shook on it.

Luke and Alex looked around, wide-eyed at all the equipment buzzing, beeping, and bubbling throughout the lab. One researcher carefully poured seawater into a glass test tube, while another clicked away at a keyboard, eyes locked on a screen filled with wavy lines and numbers. It felt like they'd stepped into a science command center. Dr. Maddox stopped outside a door with a colorful sticker that read: "Warning: Science in Progress." She gave it a soft knock.

"This is Ben," she said as the door creaked open.

Ben looked about twenty-five, with messy brown hair that stuck up as he'd just rolled out of bed, which, judging by the large coffee mug labeled "Data Beast," might've been true. He wore a faded T-shirt with a cartoon puffin holding a magnifying glass and a white lab coat splattered with tiny ink stains. A pair of earbuds dangled from his pocket like tangled spaghetti.

"Hey!" Ben said, grinning. "You must be Luke and Alex, from the boat yesterday. Dr. Maddox told me that you would be coming for a visit today."

Luke grinned. "That's us."

Ben swiveled in his chair and waved them in. "Welcome to my lair of charts, graphs, and very confused computers. I spend most of my day solving science puzzles."

Alex tilted his head. "Like jigsaw puzzles?"

"Kinda," Ben said. "But with birds and weather instead of cardboard pieces. I take all the info our field teams collect, like puffin tracking tags, nest data, and even ocean temperature; and try to make sense of it. Every bit of data is a clue, and I use it to figure out how to help the puffins survive."

Luke's eyes lit up. "I love puzzles!'

"Well, you'd love this job," Ben said, pointing to a wall of blinking screens. "Tracking puffins is like solving a living riddle. You find out where they've been, guess where they'll go next, and see how stuff like storms or ocean pollution affects their chances."

"So, science is your superpower... and puffins are your mission?" Alex asked with a smile.

"Exactly!" Ben said, laughing. "We use tiny GPS trackers to follow their migration paths. Puffins fly thousands of miles every year, and somehow, they always find their way back to the same nest. It's like they have a built-in GPS in their beaks."

Luke stepped closer to a screen that showed dots moving across a map of the North Atlantic. "That's so cool. It's like puffin treasure tracking."

Ben smiled. "Yeah. And the more we understand their journey, the more we can help protect them. Especially with climate change messing up where their food lives."

Just then, one of Ben's graphs blinked, and he groaned. "Ugh. The sardine algorithm is acting up again."

"Sardine algorithm?" Alex asked, amused.

"Long story. It involves a spilled smoothie, a keyboard, and a very cranky computer," Ben muttered.

Dr. Maddox chuckled. "Ben has a bit of a reputation for accidental chaos. But he's also one of the best data puzzle-solvers we have."

Ben gave a mock bow. "Chaos is part of the scientific process."

As Ben continued explaining, the door to the office creaked open, and a new voice joined the conversation.

"Well, I don't think he mentioned that he once tripped over a cable and almost knocked over an entire shelf of field samples," the voice teased.

They turned to see a tall young woman with a long braid and a sunhat. A rock hammer was looped through her belt, and she had a notebook in her hand.

"This is Riley Carter," Dr. Maddox said with a smile. "She's a geology student and one of the best field researchers I've worked with. She's been helping with the puffin research, too."

Riley gave them a friendly wave. "Nice to meet you guys."

Riley smiled, " You two interested in nature? Or just here for the muffins?"

Luke laughed. "Both, honestly."

"We've been on a puffin tour," Alex added. "They're amazing birds."

"Well, today, you'll get to help with something that will have a positive impact," Riley smiled. "Beach cleanup. You never know what you'll find out there." Riley added, grabbing a pair of gloves. "Last time, I found half a pirate map, a rubber duck army, and a sock that definitely wasn't mine!"

After a quick look at the tracking room, filled with screens showing GPS-tagged puffin routes, and a peek at the bird recovery area, Dr. Maddox led them outside to the van.

"We're heading to Sand Cove," she said. "It's a sheltered spot, but the currents wash up a lot of junk. Every piece we pick up is one less hazard for wildlife."

The drive to Sand Cove was short but scenic. The road wound through thick coastal woods before opening up to a rocky inlet lined with driftwood, seaweed, and sand. A few gulls circled overhead, and a seal bobbed in offshore waves. Riley passed out gloves, bags, and grabbers. "Let's see who can find the weirdest piece of trash." For the next hour, they worked the shoreline. Luke found a tangled knot of rope half-buried in kelp. Alex pulled an old sneaker from under a pile of driftwood. Riley discovered part of a lobster trap lodged in the rocks.

"Stuff like this can be hazardous," she said. "Birds get stuck in it. Even seals and turtles."

Ben wandered nearby, taking notes and logging locations on his tablet.

Alex spotted something sticking out of the sand near a clump of dried seaweed. He knelt and carefully pulled it free. It was a jagged piece of a wooden crate, the edge charred and splintered. Something white and downy was stuck to the side.

"Hey, Luke. Check this out."

Luke crouched beside him. "Is that a feather?"

Riley crouched beside the broken crate, her brow furrowed. She carefully pulled out her field tweezers and lifted the small, soft feather wedged between two splintered boards.

She held it up to the light. "Yep. Puffin feather. No mistaking it. See the black and white banding here."

Luke leaned in. "But puffins don't hang out this close to shore, do they?"

Dr. Maddox stepped closer, adjusting her sunglasses. "Not usually," she said. "Puffins nest on rocky islands, way offshore. If this feather's here, something, or someone brought it here."

Riley flipped over the crate piece, squinting at a dark spot near the edge. "Check this out—burn mark. Like from an engine or maybe a flare. Could be from a boat."

Alex's eyes lit up. "Wait, like a crate used to haul gear?"

"Maybe," Dr. Maddox said, slowly turning the wood in her hands. "Or haul something alive."

Luke blinked. "Like fish?"

"Or birds," Riley said, voice low.

Alex wrinkled his nose. "You think someone was... moving puffins?"

Dr. Maddox didn't say anything for a second. Her gaze drifted out toward the water. "It sounds far-fetched," she said finally. "But scientists don't deal in assumptions. We deal in evidence."

"But who would move puffins?" Luke asked. "That's not even a thing... is it?"

Riley hesitated. "There were rumors of illegal collectors targeting rare birds. People are paying big money for animals they're not supposed to have."

Alex frowned. "So, someone could be stealing puffins... to sell them?"

Dr. Maddox nodded slowly. "If someone's taking them off the protected islands, it would explain why the colony numbers are dropping faster than expected."

Luke looked from the feather to the charred crate. "So, we might've just found a clue?"

"More than a clue," Riley said, slipping the feather into a sample bag. "We found a puzzle piece."

"And now we need to find the rest," Dr. Maddox added. "Before someone covers their tracks."

Just then, Alex called out. "You guys are going to want to see this."

The group gathered as he held up a round, brass object. It was a compass—old, oxidized, and missing part of its glass face. The needle twitched uncertainly.

"I found it tucked between two rocks," he said. "It might be part of that old wreck grandma told us about."

Luke grinned. "The Fogbound Captain?"

Ben chuckled nervously. "You mean the ghost story?"

"More than a story," Grandma said as she stepped closer. "That captain's boat disappeared without a trace."

Dr. Maddox tucked the feather into a specimen envelope. "Let's bring these back to the lab. I want to know exactly where that feather came from."

As they walked back along the beach with their bags full of debris, the boys glanced at each other. "It feels great to help clean up the beach," said Alex. "It sure does," said Luke.

Neither spoke it, but both felt it deep down: This wasn't just about cleaning up the beach anymore.

Something bigger was happening. The discovery of the feather was their first clue, and though they couldn't yet see where it would lead, they both knew one thing for sure: this was only the beginning.

Chapter 5 – Climbs and Conversations

Uncle John was a man of few words. Still, it was usually worth listening to when he spoke, especially if he told one of his wild stories. Tall and thin, with bright blue eyes that could twinkle with mischief, Uncle John made even the simplest things seem exciting. He was the kind of guy who could always find a way to keep you on your toes.

Uncle John lived next door to Grandma Maggie in a house as neat as a pin, just like him. His yard looked like it was straight out of a postcard, with rows of flower beds and trimmed hedges that could've been drawn with a ruler. Everything was in its place, down to the last pebble. Luke and Alex loved to pop over to John's house on a hot summer day and sip on his homemade root beer soda.

Before he became the steady, reliable presence in Bar Harbor, he was a sailor who spent his days navigating the treacherous waters along the Maine coastline. He and his brother, Tom, had worked together for years, braving the wild seas in search of adventure and whatever treasure or challenge the ocean threw their way. But after Thomas passed away, John didn't take to the sea as much. Instead, he found his adventure in looking after Grandma Maggie and her family.

Luke and Alex always knew Uncle John would drop everything to help, fixing the boat dock, building a bonfire, or giving a friendly nudge to anyone needing direction. He didn't make a big deal about it. He didn't need to. He was always there, quietly watching, with those sharp blue eyes, ensuring everything ran smoothly.

And then there were the nights when Uncle John would pop over for a game of cards or sit by the bonfire with Grandma Maggie, telling tall tales about the sea. He had a way of making the mundane seem magical. His campfire ghost stories were legendary, and his stories recounting old shipwrecks were always a highlight. He seemed to have a way of making you feel like you were part of the adventure!

The sun rose over Bar Harbor the next morning, creating bright streaks of pink and orange. The air was crisp and fresh, a perfect day for a hike. The scent of saltwater and pine filled the morning air, a reminder of the natural beauty surrounding them.

Luke and Alex had barely finished breakfast when Grandma Maggie appeared, packing a sturdy daypack with water, sandwiches, and a batch of her famous lemon blueberry bars. This treat always made their mouths water. "And don't forget," she said, handing Luke a small trail map, "stay on the marked paths. Acadia has its moods."

Luke nodded eagerly as he buckled the straps of his backpack. "Got it, Grandma. We'll stick to the trail. We don't want to get lost near Bubble Rock, right?"

Grandma chuckled. "It's a lot harder to get lost on a well-marked trail, but with Bubble Rock, you never know. Just remember to enjoy the journey."

"Are you sure you do not want to join us?" asked Alex.

"Oh," smiled Grandma Maggie, "I would love to, but I have a pottery order to fill. I'll be sure to join one of your next hikes!"

Before they could say another word, a familiar rumble of an engine came from the driveway. Luke and Alex both rushed to the window and saw Uncle John's old, reliable pickup truck pulling up. His vehicle, as neat as everything else in his life, had fishing gear in the back, always arranged carefully, like he'd been preparing for some unspoken adventure.

Uncle John stepped out, wearing his usual Maine cap, looking like he'd just stepped out of the pages of a local travel guide. His walking stick was firmly gripped in his hand, a tool he'd carried for as long as the boys could remember. "Morning, boys!" he called, his voice deep and steady. "Ready to stretch those legs and get to Bubble Rock?"

Luke grinned. "We've been ready for this hike since we got here. You sure you're up for it, Uncle John?"

Uncle John gave a sly smile, his blue eyes twinkling. "I've been up to Bubble Rock more times than I can count, but it's always worth it. The air smells like sea and secrets today. Let's go."

Alex grabbed his jacket and slung his backpack over his shoulders. "I'll race you to the truck," he challenged Luke, already running toward the driveway.

Luke laughed, calling back to Uncle John, "You know I'll beat him."

Uncle John chuckled as he made his way to the truck. "All right, all right, you two, let's get going. I've got a few stories saved up for this trip. Did I ever tell you about the honey incident of '92?"

Uncle John began, leaning back in his seat, eyes twinkling. Uncle John waved to Maggie as they drove away. "I was deep in the White Mountains, hiking solo with nothing but a backpack, a compass, and a jar of wildflower honey I'd picked up from a roadside stand." Luke and Alex leaned in.

"I'd just set up camp and was digging a fire ring when I heard it, a twig snap. Not a squirrel snap. Not a raccoon scuffle. A big 'some-things coming' kind of snap."

He paused dramatically.

"I looked up, and there it was. A black bear. Not ten feet away. Eyes on my backpack. Or more specifically... my honey jar."

Alex's eyes went wide. "Did it charge?"

"Nope," Uncle John said. "Worse. It outsmarted me."

Luke blinked. "What do you mean?"

"That bear looked me dead in the eye, then sat down. Just plopped its fuzzy behind right there and stared. And then, get this, it tilted its head like it was thinking. And I swear to you, that bear smirked."

"Smirked?" Alex laughed.

"Yup. Next thing I know, it grabs a stick—A STICK!—and uses it to drag my backpack closer. I was so stunned I didn't even move. It unzipped the pack with one claw, like it had done this a hundred times before, and pulled out the honey. Then it sauntered off into the woods, not a care in the world. But before it disappeared, it turned back and burped. Loud."

"What did you do?" Luke asked.

"I hiked all the way back down the mountain hungry and humbled," Uncle John said with a sigh. Luke and Alex rolled with laughter from the back seat as they pictured the honey-loving bear!

The road to the Bubble Rock trailhead wound through Acadia's forests and open meadows, past rocky cliffs and patches of wildflowers. The boys could feel the anticipation building. This wasn't just any hike; this was the start of another adventure, a tradition, and a chance to see Bubble Rock, the famous balancing rock at the top of the mountain, up close.

As they continued the drive, Uncle John pointed out landmarks, hidden trails, interesting rock formations, and places he'd taken the boys on previous hikes. It was clear he had a deep connection to this place. To Uncle John, this wasn't just a park; it was home.

When they reached the trailhead to South Bubble, Luke stepped out of the truck and looked around in awe. The towering granite ridges rose on either side, the scent of spruce and moss thick in the air. Ferns carpeted the forest floor, and the sound of distant waterfalls trickled through the trees.

"This is Bubble Rock Trail," Uncle John said, shouldering a pack. "Steady climb, but the views are worth it. Bubble Rock is a glacial erratic, a giant traveler from the Ice Age, dropped right where it sits by a slow-moving glacier thousands of years ago."

They began the hike, winding up switchbacks lined with boulders and exposed roots. The climb was tough, and the boys could feel their legs start to burn as they made their way up the trail. Each step felt more challenging than the last, but the closer they got to the top, the more pumped they became. The air was fresh and crisp, while the forest buzzed with birds calling and leaves rustling in the breeze.

As they climbed higher, the view kept getting better. They could see shimmering lakes below, jagged mountain peaks stretching into the distance, and wild blueberry bushes scattered across the hillside, dotting it like nature's treasure map. Luke pointed to a bush. "Wild blueberries?"

Uncle John squinted at the plant and then turned to the boys with a mock-serious expression. "How can you be sure they're blueberries? They might be something else, poisonous even."

Alex crouched to examine the leaves. "Oval leaves with smooth edges. Five-pointed star on the bottom of the berry. Grows low to the ground. We know how to identify them."

Uncle John grinned. "Just testing you. Ayuh, those are blueberries, all right. You pass the test."

Luke popped one in his mouth. "Tart, but good!"

"Hey!" A familiar voice rang out. "I thought I might run into you two!" Riley sat on a flat rock, sketching the landscape in a notebook. She stood, brushing dust from her pants. Her sunhat was clipped to her pack, and a rock sample bag swung at her hip.

"You're hiking Bubble, too?" Alex asked.

"Of course," she said. "The geology here is incredible. See that ridge over there?" She pointed. "That's Cadillac Mountain granite, formed over 400 million years ago. This whole region is a geologist's dream. There's volcanic rock, sandstone, ancient ocean sediment... and some of the best glacial features on the East Coast."

Luke raised his eyebrows. "What got you into rocks?"

Riley smiled. "My dad gave me a geode when I was five. I cracked it open and saw crystals inside; it felt like opening a secret. Ever since then, I have wanted to understand what makes the Earth tick."

They hiked together the rest of the way. Riley pointed out feldspar veins, quartz pockets, and polished glacial striations along the granite. "The glaciers that carved this park moved boulders the size of houses," she said. "They left behind kettle ponds, erratics, and U-shaped valleys. It's all a story in stone."

When they finally reached Bubble Rock, the boys froze. Perched on the cliff's edge was a massive boulder, round and smooth, like it had no business sitting there. One firm push, it seemed, and it would tumble down the mountain.

"It's not going anywhere," Riley said, laughing at their expressions. "Glaciers put it there, and gravity's been trying to move it ever since."

They sat near the edge, munching on dried fruit and watching the morning stretch into bright sunshine. The view went on forever, sparkling lakes below them, dark green pine forests, and, far away, the ocean dotted with tiny islands.

As they ate, Riley flipped open her notebook again. "I wanted to tell you something important," she said. "Dr. Maddox tested the feather we found."

Everyone leaned closer.

"She said it was fresh," Riley continued. "It didn't fall out on its own, and it wasn't taken by a predator. The feather came from a live puffin."

Alex frowned. "Then how did it come loose?"

Riley tapped her pencil against the page. "Dr. Maddox thinks the bird was inside a wooden crate. The feather got caught between the boards and pulled free when the puffin moved."

The group fell quiet.

"So... someone put a puffin in a crate?" Alex asked.

"Possibly for research," Riley said, but her voice wobbled just a little. She didn't sound sure.

"I think we should go back to the Research Center and talk to Dr. Maddox," Alex said. "There's more going on here."

Luke nodded. "I want to understand what's happening to the puffins, and why anyone would be messing with them."

Uncle John smiled and stood up, brushing off his hands. "Well, that sounds like a plan. We can give Riley a ride back to the Research Center," he said, already reaching for the car keys.

Uncle John eased the truck onto the main road, the sound of gravel crunching under the tires filling the quiet. Luke leaned back, still feeling the burn in his legs from the climb, but the excitement of the hike kept his energy up. Looking out the window, Alex seemed to be lost in thought, probably trying to piece together everything they had learned so far.

"You know," Uncle John shrugged, glancing in the rearview mirror, "there's this great little place on the way to the center. Best lobster rolls you'll ever have. What do you say we stop for lunch?"

Riley grinned. "Sounds perfect. I could go for a break, and I'm starving!"

The truck turned off the main road onto a smaller dirt path that led to a quaint seafood shack with a view of the harbor. The wooden sign out front read "Breezy's Lobster Shack." The air smelled of a fresh sea breeze, mingled with the promise of delicious food. The place was cozy, with a few picnic tables scattered outside and a line of customers chatting with the owner behind the counter.

They parked, stretching their legs after the long hike. As they walked up to the shack, Luke couldn't help but smile at the weathered building. There was something so comforting about places like this, small, unassuming, and full of local charm.

Uncle John led the way up to the counter. "Four lobster rolls, a couple of chowders, and let's see... how about a round of fries, too?" he asked, already knowing the order.

Riley chuckled. "And two orders of those homemade blueberry pies to go," she added.

The owner, an older man with a white beard and a cap that read "Catch of the Day," smiled. "Good choice. You won't regret it."

They sat outside, the salty breeze tugging at their sleeves as waves crashed against the rocky shore. Seagulls cried overhead, looking for anyone willing to share a fry. The rich, buttery taste of Maine's famous lobster rolls still lingered on their tongues. Uncle John wiped a bit of mayo from the corner of his mouth and leaned back with a grin. "You boys ever hear the *real* story of how the lobster roll came to be?"

Luke shook his head. "There's a real story?"

"Oh, sure," Uncle John chuckled, lowering his voice like he was letting them in on a secret. "It all started back in the 1920s in a tiny seaside joint in Milford, Connecticut. There was this guy, let's call him Harry Perry. Owned a little restaurant where the floors squeaked, and the seagulls stole your fries if you looked away too long. Anyway, one day, a customer walks in, a big guy, hungry like a bear after hibernation, and says, "Harry, I want lobster, but not on a plate. I want it in a sandwich. Something I can eat with one hand while I steer my car with the other!"

Luke's eyes widened. "Wait, people drove while eating lobster back then?"

"Not without getting lobster all over the place," Uncle John said with a laugh. "But Harry was a clever guy. He scooped up chunks of hot, butter-dripping lobster, piled them high between soft buns, and turned a messy feast into something you could actually eat on the road." The man takes one bite and nearly drives off the road from joy! And just like that, the lobster roll was born."

Alex grinned. "That can't be real."

"Oh, it's real all right," Uncle John said, wagging a French fry for emphasis. "Now, at first, they used regular white bread. But that got soggy faster than my boots in a marsh. So, someone, and I suspect it was a genius baker with a sandwich obsession, came up with the split-top bun. A bun with a pocket. Like a lobster sleeping bag."

"Gross," Luke laughed.

"Delicious," Uncle John corrected. "And here's the best part, some people eat 'em warm with butter, some cold with mayo. It caused so many arguments in New England, I'm pretty sure it nearly started the Great Lobster Civil War of 1937."

"There was no..." Alex began,

But Uncle John just winked and interrupted. "So, the next time you bite into a lobster roll," he said, lifting his roll, "remember Harry Perry, his hungry customer, and the brave sandwich that changed seafood forever."

Luke and Alex rolled with laughter.

Laughter had faded into thoughtful silence as they climbed back into the truck, their bellies full but their minds buzzing with questions. The Research Center was just a few minutes away, but the air inside the cab felt heavier with each passing mile. Something was brewing. And if anyone had the clues to unlock it, it was Dr. Maddox.

Chapter 6 – A Theory No One Wanted to Believe

The cool air of the research center was a sharp contrast to the heat of the day as the group filed into Dr. Maddox's office. She looked up from her desk, her expression shifting from focus to recognition. "Ah, Luke, Alex, and Uncle John! And Riley, too! I didn't expect to see you all here today," she said, her voice welcoming, with a touch of excitement. "What brings you in today?"

Luke spoke first, eager to get to the heart of the mystery. "We have been thinking more about the feather we found the other day, and wanted to learn more about the puffins. You know why anyone would want to mess with them? Is there something special about puffins that makes them valuable?"

Dr. Maddox motioned for them to sit. "That's a good question. Puffins, especially here in Maine, are vital to the ecosystem. They help control fish populations and are also indicators of the health of our marine environment. They're a key part of the food web." She paused, her fingers drumming the desk as she looked at the boys, her expression turning serious. "But here's the thing, puffins aren't just important to the environment but also valuable in pretty terrible ways. People sometimes steal their feathers, eggs, and even the birds to sell them illegally. Some people collect all types of animals as exotic pets, including puffins. This is a big problem for many species.

"Alex's eyebrows shot up, and his mouth dropped open. "Wait, people actually steal puffins and sell them?"

Dr. Maddox nodded slowly. "Sadly, yes. It's rare, but it happens. Puffins are tough little birds, but they're vulnerable too, and some people will do anything to make a quick buck, even if it means hurting the puffin population in the process." She leaned forward, her voice softening. "That's why we're so careful with them. We do everything we can to protect them."

Uncle John, who had been listening quietly, shifted in his seat. "Well, Dr. Maddox, that is very disturbing. What can we do to help?"

Dr. Maddox sighed, looking down at her hands for a moment. "It's not easy. The best we can do is ensure the puffin nests are closely monitored, and people stay away from the colonies. We also try to educate the public about their importance, so they understand what's at stake. But it's a constant battle. There's always someone looking to profit off nature."

Luke glanced at Uncle John. "That explains a lot... but who would do something like that around here?"

Before anyone could respond, a voice from the back of the room interrupted them. Ben, the young researcher, walked in with a stack of papers. "Sorry if I am interrupting," he smiled, setting the papers on Dr. Maddox's desk.

"Hey, Ben," Riley said, raising an eyebrow and looking in his direction. "We were just talking about puffins. You work on the puffin tracking data, right?"

Ben smiled quickly, but it didn't quite reach his eyes. "Yeah, that's right, how can I help you?" Ben replied.

"We are very concerned about the population decline and a potential trafficking involvement," said Dr. Maddox.

Ben looked stunned. "Trafficking?" he replied. "That sounds a bit far-fetched, don't you think? I just put the new data I collected on your desk. I haven't noticed anything alarming in my research," said Ben.

Dr. Maddox looked at Ben, her fingers lightly tapping the desk. "We just have reason to be concerned; nothing is concrete. We need to keep a close watch on their nests, the hatchling numbers, and migration paths. Ben, if you notice anything in your research that looks off, I want you to let me know immediately!"

Ben hesitated, his gaze shifting as if unsure whether to speak. Finally, he spoke, his voice quieter. "I will, Dr. Maddox. I... I know it's probably unrelated, but I've seen something strange lately. A few weeks ago, I saw this old fisherman out by the cliffs near the lighthouse. He looked like he was scouting the area, looking for something. Didn't think much of it at first, but... his behavior just seemed odd. I think his name's Eli. Eli Jensen."

Uncle John's demeanor immediately shifted when Eli was mentioned. His usually warm blue eyes grew cold, and he looked directly at Ben. The room seemed to hold its breath. "Eli Jensen?" Uncle John's voice was low, almost a growl. "Are you sure it was Eli?"

Ben hesitated before speaking, his voice a little lower than usual. "Look, I've seen Eli hanging around the cliffs near the lighthouse lately, but it's not like he's just walking by. He's been more... deliberate. Staring at the rocks, studying the ground like he's trying to figure something out. I caught him peering at an old, weathered piece of wood washed up on the shore, like he was trying to make out some old markings on it. It was strange. I didn't think much of it at the time, but now I'm not so sure."

The room fell silent for a beat as they all considered Ben's words. Dr. Maddox glanced toward Uncle John, catching the flicker of something dark behind his eyes.

"You know him," she said quietly. "What's the story with Eli Jensen?"

Uncle John didn't respond right away. He stared out the window, jaw tight, a muscle twitching near his temple. "Eli and I worked together years ago, marine salvage operations, up and down the coast. He was good at what he did, no doubt about that. But he had a habit of bending the rules. Always looking for a loophole, a way to make fast money. Eventually, it caught up with him. He lost his license and got into some shady dealings."

Luke and Alex exchanged a quick glance, the air around them growing heavier.

Dr. Maddox frowned. "You think he could be involved in this?"

"I think," Uncle John said slowly, turning back to face them, "that Eli doesn't do anything without a reason. If he's sniffing around the cliffs and poking at driftwood, he's not out there for a stroll."

Ben shifted uncomfortably. "Look, I don't know for sure that Eli's involved. It's just... something I noticed. He's been in and out of the area lately, and he's not exactly someone I'd trust."

Uncle John stared at Ben for a long moment, his eyes sharp, calculating. Then he turned back to Dr. Maddox. "Well, I think we've got our work cut out for us," he said, his tone cooler than before. "We'll keep an eye on things. And if Eli's involved, I'll deal with it."

Luke, Alex, and waved goodbye to Uncle John as he drove back home. Before heading home themselves, the boys had a mission to complete for Grandma Maggie. It was a beautiful walk through downtown Bar Harbor, past all the little shops with flower boxes in the windows and the smell of sea air mixed with fudge and sunscreen. Halfway down Main Street, they couldn't resist stopping at Scoops Ahoy, their favorite ice cream shop. Luke went straight for his usual wild Maine blueberry in a waffle cone, while Alex debated for a full minute before settling on mint chip. They sat on the little bench out front, swinging their legs and watching people pass by with beach towels and shopping bags, the sun warm on their backs.

After finishing their ice cream, they walked to Captain Red's dock. The cries of seagulls and the gentle rhythm of waves brushing against the boat wrapped them in a familiar, comforting calm. Captain Red spotted them as they approached. He waved them over with a grin, his hands busy organizing the lines for the lobster crates.

"Well, look who's here!" he called, his voice booming across the water. "What can I do for you boys today?"

Alex waved back. "We need some fresh lobsters for Grandma Maggie. She said you're the man to talk to."

Captain Red let out a hearty laugh. "You bet I am! Give me a minute, I'll have them ready for you." He bent down to haul a crate from the boat, the smell of saltwater and seafood mixing in the air. "Nothing beats fresh lobsters right from the boat. You boys enjoying your stay here in Bar Harbor?"

Luke and Alex exchanged glances.

"Actually," Luke started, "we've been trying to figure out what's happening around here. Have you noticed anything strange going on around here? Maybe something on the water or near the cliffs?"

Captain Red paused, looking over at them with a more serious expression. He stopped pulling lobsters and placed the crate down. His eyes narrowed slightly as he seemed to think back on something. "Well, now that you mention it," he said slowly, "I've been seeing some weird stuff lately. Not just around the docks, but out on the water... near the old lighthouse."

Alex leaned in. "What kind of stuff?"

Captain Red glanced around, almost like he was making sure no one was listening. "I don't like to talk too much about it, but I was out on the water a couple of weeks ago when a storm had just passed. I saw something strange, a flash of light at the top of the lighthouse. It wasn't like a regular light. Captain Red paused momentarily, his eyes narrowing as he recalled the strange sight. "It was quick, like someone shining a flashlight from up there. Could've been a trick of the light, but I've been around long enough to know what I saw."

Luke and Alex exchanged surprised glances. "A flash of light?" Luke asked, still trying to wrap his head around it. "But the lighthouse has been abandoned for years."

"Yeah, that's what I thought too," Captain Red said, wiping his hands on a rag. "But that's the only explanation. Could've been a signal, or maybe someone's up there messing around." He shook his head, looking out toward the lighthouse, his expression unreadable. "Whatever it was, it doesn't sit right." Who knows? Maybe...it was the ghost of the Captain of the Seabird, lost long ago in a storm off the coast!" he chuckled and winked at the boys.

"Thanks, Captain," Luke said, grinning with excitement. "We'll keep an eye out. And thanks for the lobsters! I bet they are going to be delicious."

Captain Red chuckled, handing them the bag of fresh lobsters. "You boys take care of yourselves now and keep an eye on that lighthouse. It's seen more than its fair share of strange happenings."

The boys exchanged a quick glance, and their hearts skipped a beat.

"Do you really think there could be a ghost?" Luke said, raising an eyebrow and trying to act casual.

"Wouldn't surprise me," Captain Red teased, winking at them.

With the bag of lobsters in hand, the boys walked back to Grandma Maggie's house, buzzing with energy. The idea of a ghostly sea captain had their imaginations running wild. A flash of light at the lighthouse? That was their lead, and they were itching to investigate.

Chapter 7 – Equipment, Questions, and a Signal in the Dark

The evening air in Bar Harbor was warm, and the scent of freshly steamed lobster filled the kitchen as Luke and Alex sat down at Grandma Maggie's table. The table had all the fixings for a proper lobster dinner: steamed lobster, corn on the cob, boiled potatoes, and a big bowl of Grandma's homemade coleslaw. Bear was lounging near the table, his eyes half-closed as if he knew something delicious was about to happen.

Alex cracked open a lobster, his fingers red from the heat, and glanced at Luke. "I can't believe Captain Red also said he saw flashes of light from the lighthouse. He said it was like someone was up there with a flashlight or something."

Luke's eyes widened as he cracked his own lobster. "That's what I thought! When I saw it during the puffin cruise, I figured it was just a trick of the light, but then Captain Red mentioned it and... well, now it's got me thinking. It can't be a coincidence."

They looked at Grandma Maggie, who had been listening quietly while dipping her lobster in melted butter. Her eyes twinkled with curiosity. "So, you two have seen something strange at the lighthouse, huh?" Grandma asked, her voice thoughtful.

Luke nodded. "Yeah, just a flash of light, the same as Captain Red described. With all that has been going on with the puffins, well, I guess we are curious to see if it is somehow connected."

Grandma leaned back in her chair, folding her arms. "A flash, huh? That's interesting." She smiled, "So, have you devised a plan?"

Alex glanced at Luke. "Well, we were thinking about heading out there. We could ride our bikes and see if we catch another flash or maybe notice something strange. We are just going to watch, that's all. We will be careful." Grandma's smile widened just a little, but it wasn't the kind of smile that said she was surprised. "Ah, I see. And you two think you can ride out there and handle it all alone?" She raised an eyebrow, clearly amused.

"Well... yeah," Luke said, shrugging.

Grandma chuckled softly. She knew her grandsons, and when their curiosity was piqued, there wasn't much she could do to distract them. "I've got some old gear that might help you out. It's nothing new, but it's still reliable." She stood up and walked to a closet near the back door, pulling out a few items.

Alex asked curiously. "What kind of gear?" Grandma pulled out a pair of old, yet surprisingly high-tech binoculars for their time, along with a vintage spotting scope and a small handheld radio. "I've had these for years," she said, handing the binoculars to Luke and the scope to Alex. "Used them back when I did some research of my own, don't laugh," she added, sensing their surprise. "This stuff still works, and it'll help you keep an eye on things from a safe distance."

Luke's eyes widened as he examined the binoculars. "Wow, these are pretty cool!"

Grandma looked at them both knowingly. "You two are always up to something. Just make sure you keep in touch. I don't need to tell you to be careful out there."

Alex nodded. "We'll be careful, Grandma."

"Keep me posted. "Oh, and take these," she added, handing each a flashlight. "Text me when you get there."

As the boys headed toward the door, ready to grab their bikes, Grandma's voice stopped them, "Oh, and don't forget to check in regularly," she said. "If you see anything that feels even a little bit wrong, you call me right away."

The boys nodded, excitement buzzing between them. They weren't sure what they'd find at the lighthouse, but they were determined to figure it out, and with Grandma's gear, they might actually have a chance.

Luke glanced down at the binoculars in his hand, then looked up, puzzled. "Wait... how did you get these, Grandma?"

Grandma's smile curled into something knowing. "Let's just say they came in handy back when I did a bit of surveillance myself."

Alex's head snapped up. "You did surveillance?"

"Nothing too exciting," Grandma said lightly, though her eyes sparkled. "Just paying close attention when it mattered."

Luke exchanged a look with Alex. "Paying attention to what?" Luke pressed.

Grandma only laughed and gave a small shrug. "Oh, you know. Things that didn't quite add up."

Alex raised an eyebrow. "That doesn't sound like nothing."

Grandma leaned forward and wrapped her arms around both boys before they could ask more. "You boys have such an imagination," she said, giving them a playful wink. Then she hugged them tightly. "Just remember, be smart, be careful, and stick together. I love you both."

Luke grinned, feeling the thrill rise in his chest. "We love you too, Grandma. Don't worry, we've got it all under control."

Grandma laughed softly, but she didn't answer their questions. The twinkle in her eye told them one thing for sure: There was definitely more to Grandma's story than she was letting on.

As the night settled in, the boys grabbed their parents' mountain bikes, which they had done for years. The bikes were old, but sturdy enough for a quick ride to the lighthouse. As they pedaled away from Grandma's house, the streetlights of Bar Harbor flickered out behind them, and the quiet of the night wrapped around them.

"Ready for this?" Luke asked, looking over at Alex as they cruised down the hill.

Alex grinned. "Are you kidding? We've been waiting for this." The wheels spun faster as the boys rode toward the lighthouse, their excitement matching the rhythm of the bikes. They had a mystery to solve, and this time, they were ready to uncover whatever secrets the lighthouse was hiding.

The moon was high above, casting long shadows over the forest as Luke and Alex rode toward the bluff. The night air smelled of saltwater and pine, and a chill settled over the land as the sun dipped below the horizon. Their minds buzzed with the day's events, and they couldn't shake the memory of the flashes of light Captain Red had seen from the lighthouse.

"Do you think we'll see the light?" Alex asked, pulling his jacket tighter around his shoulders as the wind picked up off the water.

"I hope so," Luke said, his voice buzzing with excitement. "If that flash wasn't just a fluke, there could be more, and maybe we will find a connection to the puffin mystery."

They reached the top of the bluff, taking in the sweeping view of Frenchman Bay below. The old, weathered lighthouse stood like a shadow against the night sky, its jagged silhouette barely visible in the silver moonlight. Built to guide ships safely through the treacherous Maine waters, the lighthouse was once a beacon of hope and safety for sailors navigating the dark, stormy seas.

But now the black glass of the tower seemed to shimmer, reflecting the pale light as though it were alive, watching them in return. Luke's heart pounded as he settled in and adjusted the binoculars, his gaze fixed on the looming structure, hoping to catch another flash. Every nerve in his body was on alert, waiting and hoping for the light to reappear.

"Ready?" Luke asked, his voice barely a whisper as he turned to Alex, excitement written all over his face.

Alex nodded, adjusting the small spotting scope they'd borrowed from Grandma Maggie. It was an old piece of equipment, but it worked well enough for their needs. He pointed it toward the lighthouse. "Any sign?"

Luke trained his binoculars on the dark structure. "Not yet," he said.

Alex and Luke stood in silence; their eyes fixed on the lighthouse. The spruce trees around them creaked and swayed with the breeze, their branches brushing against each other, while the distant roar of waves crashing against the jagged rocks below was the only sound breaking the stillness. The world seemed to hold its breath as the minutes ticked, each second dragging on with intense anticipation.

Then, without warning, Luke's voice sliced through the quiet night. "There!" he whispered urgently, his heart racing with excitement. "A flash!"

Alex quickly adjusted the scope, zooming in on the lighthouse. "Short flash... What do you think it is? That wasn't natural." And then...more flashes.

Luke's eyes lit up with realization. "I wonder if it could be Morse code. I learned it last fall during wilderness training. Hand me the notebook."

Alex looked at him in surprise. "Morse code? You sure?"

Luke didn't take his eyes off the lighthouse. "They're using light signals, not just flashing for fun. If they're doing something shady, it makes sense to use something that can't be traced."

Alex paused for a second before grabbing the notebook from his backpack and passing it to Luke with a pen. "You know, Morse code was developed back in 1830. We live in a modern world. Why wouldn't they just use phones?"

Luke shook his head, scanning the lighthouse with intense focus. "Too risky. If they're poaching puffins or doing something illegal, phones leave a trail. GPS tracking and call logs are all recorded. If the police catch them, it's all evidence."

"Have you been watching True Crime TV with your mom again?" Alex teased. Alex adjusted the scope, narrowing his eyes as the old lighthouse flickered in the distance. "Short flash... pause... three quick flashes... That doesn't look like the normal rotation."

Luke leaned forward. "That wasn't random. Did you see that rhythm?"

More flashes came; three, then two, then a long one. Luke grabbed his notebook and started scribbling. Luke said. "This isn't Morse Code; it doesn't match. It's too clean. Morse is all dots and dashes, short and long pulses. This is... something else."

Alex frowned. "Weird. Maybe it's a broken bulb?"

Luke shook his head. "No way. It's repeating. Same sequence. Look, here it goes again."

Flash... flash-flash-flash... pause... flash-flash... pause... flash...

Luke wrote it down as **3 − 4 − 1 − 5 − 6 − 2 − 5 − 3 − 1.**

"It's like they're counting," Alex said. "But why?"

They sat in silence, staring out over the dark water as the light repeated its strange message. Seagulls cried faintly overhead. The sea was calm, but something about the rhythm of the flashes made Luke's skin prickle.

"I don't get it," Alex said. "It's not Morse. It's not letters. How are we going to figure this out?"

Luke tapped his pencil against the notebook. "I'm not sure, but I bet Grandma Maggie can help."

"I'm gonna copy down the full sequence," Luke said. "Then we show Grandma Maggie. If anyone can help us figure this out, it's her."

Back at the house, they burst through the side door and into the mudroom. Bear yawned from his perch on the windowsill, then jumped down and padded silently after them. Grandma was in the kitchen, peeling apples for a pie.

"You boys look like you've seen a ghost," she said.

"Worse," Luke said, tossing the notebook on the table. "We saw a code."

"A light code," Alex added. "Coming from the lighthouse."

Grandma glanced at the page. "That's not Morse," she said right away.

Luke raised an eyebrow. "You know Morse?"

Grandma smiled mysteriously. "I know a lot of things. What matters is what you've found here... It's numbers. Sequences. That means it's probably encoded using something older, something physical."

She wiped her hands on a towel, then disappeared through the door and headed out into the garage.

A few minutes later, she returned with a long, velvet-lined wooden box. She opened it slowly, revealing a strange metal cylinder made of disks, each one with scrambled letters etched around the edge.

Luke leaned in, eyes wide. "What is that thing?"

It's called a Bazeries Cylinder," Grandma said, setting the strange metal object on the table with a soft *clink*.

The boys leaned in. The cylinder was made of smooth, silvery metal and looked like a stack of thick rings slid onto a rod. Each ring was etched with tiny letters that wrapped all the way around, and they spun freely with a quiet *click-click* when Grandma turned them.

"It was invented more than a hundred years ago," Grandma went on. "Long before computers or secret passwords. Back then, if you wanted to send a message no one else could read, you used something clever, like this." She twisted the rings, and the letters scrambled into nonsense.

"We used something like it in the field."

"In the *field*?" Alex repeated, raising an eyebrow.

Grandma smiled, slow and sly. "Let's just say it came in handy back when I was working on... very complicated paperwork." She gave them a wink.

Luke frowned at the spinning letters. "So, what does it do?"

"Well," Grandma said, tapping the cylinder, "you line up the disks in just the right order, and suddenly the jumble of letters turns into real words. It's how people used to hide messages from prying eyes, during wars, expeditions, and important missions."

She leaned closer, lowering her voice like she was sharing a secret. "If you don't know the right order, the message looks like gibberish. But get it right..." She spun the rings one last time and smiled. "Poof, secrets spill out like jam from a broken jar."

Alex and Luke stared at the cylinder, their imaginations racing.

Luke whispered, "Did you use it to send messages?"

Grandma just chuckled and slid the cylinder back toward them. "All I'll say is this," she said. "It's amazing what people will write down when they think no one else can read it."

The boys exchanged a look. Whatever Grandma had really done, it sounded a lot more exciting than paperwork.

Alex blinked. "And you've just had this in the garage?"

"It was under the box of Christmas ornaments," she said casually, like it was no big deal.

Luke held up his notebook. "The numbers from the lighthouse, can this thing decode them?"

"If you have the key," Grandma said with a nod.

"And we don't," Alex pointed out.

"Not yet," she said. "But if that message is real, the key must be out there. Whoever's sending those flashes has a plan. People don't use something this old unless they want to stay completely off the radar."

Luke felt a chill ripple down his back. "So, what do we do?"

Grandma looked at both boys, then gently closed the lid on the cipher. "We find the key," she said, her voice low but certain. "And when we do, we find out exactly what they're trying to hide."

The smell of sizzling bacon and buttermilk pancakes pulled Luke out of a restless sleep. Sunlight streamed through the curtains, and somewhere downstairs, Bear let out a dramatic yawn. Luke sat up, rubbing his eyes. His brain felt like it had been running laps all night.

By the time he and Alex shuffled into the kitchen, Grandma Maggie was already flipping pancakes like a breakfast ninja. A stack of golden, fluffy discs steamed beside a bowl of fresh blueberries. The cat had claimed a chair and was watching the spatula's movements as if it were a tennis match.

"Morning, boys," Grandma said cheerfully. She wore a red apron with a puffin stitched across the front and had her gray hair tied up in a bun that somehow still looked adventurous.

"Morning," Luke mumbled, sliding into his seat. "I couldn't sleep," he said after a beat. "I kept tossing and turning, trying to figure out what the keyword could be for the cipher."

"I was dreaming about rotating metal disks," Alex added, reaching for the syrup. "And one of them turned into a cookie halfway through."

Grandma chuckled. "Let's see if breakfast gives your brains a little boost."

After they ate, the boys pulled the Bazeries Cylinder out of its box and laid it across the table. They opened Luke's notebook with the message numbers and got to work.

"Let's try 'Stormwatch' first," Luke said. "That's the lighthouse."

No luck.

"'Lobster'?" Alex tried. "We're in Maine."

Nothing made sense.

"'Harbor'? 'Feather'? 'Eggs'?"

More gibberish.

Luke groaned and slumped forward. "It's like spinning a combination lock when you don't even know how many numbers there are."

"Keep trying," Grandma encouraged, rinsing dishes behind them. "Sometimes the answer's right in front of you, waiting for the moment you're ready to see it."

Just then, the phone rang, sharp and sudden, cutting through the quiet like a dropped coin in a still room. Grandma picked it up, her expression shifting subtly as she listened. "Hello... Oh, hi, Evelyn. Yes... I see. Alright, I'll tell them."

She hung up and turned to the boys, her voice calm but her eyes glinting with an unreadable look. "Dr. Maddox wants to see you right away."

The boys rolled into the gravel lot outside the Bar Harbor Research Center, their bikes crunching to a stop. The breeze off the harbor carried the scent of salt and seaweed.

Riley met them at the side door, her ponytail pulled through a ball cap, clipboard in hand. "Glad you made it," she said, opening the door. "Dr. Maddox has something to show you. She said it's strange."

Luke tilted his head. "Why does she want us?"

Riley gave him a look. "You're the ones who found the crate, that's why we need your help now."

They exchanged a glance and followed her inside. The lab was cool and brightly lit, filled with the soft hum of machines. Dr. Maddox was at a stainless steel table, the charred piece of crate lay out in front of her under a bright lamp.

"I've been analyzing the wood," she said without looking up. "Fish protein, salt, oil, all expected. But under the burn..." She gently rotated the plank. "We found this."

Etched into the wood, half-hidden beneath the soot, was a symbol: a three-pointed compass rose with jagged spokes and a curved wave slashing across the center. Above the top spoke, a small dot had been carved with precision.

"That's not on any registry," Dr. Maddox continued. "No company stamp I know of."

Riley leaned in. "Definitely not local. Looks more like a logo than a shipping mark."

Alex's brow furrowed. "Hang on. That looks really familiar."

He pulled out his phone and began scrolling quickly.

"What are you doing?" Luke asked.

"Remember when you were trying to balance that lobster trap on your head at the docks?"

Luke groaned. "Please tell me you didn't save that picture."

"Of course I saved it," Alex laughed. "But look, right here."

He turned the phone around. In the background of the photo, half-hidden by fencing and coiled rope, sat a dusty wooden crate. The same symbol was burned into its side.

"There it is," Riley said. "Same mark."

"And look under it," Alex said. "See that? It says Trailbend Equipment Division."

Luke's eyes lit up. "Trailbend. That could be the key."

"Key to what?" Dr. Maddox asked, now watching them both closely.

Luke took a breath, "We haven't told you everything. A few nights ago, we were watching the old Stormwatch lighthouse."

"But Stormwatch has been shut down for years," Riley commented, curious.

"Not that night," Alex said. "We saw flashes of light. In a pattern. At first, we thought it was Morse code, but it didn't match."

Luke pulled a crumpled page from the pocket of his hoodie. "We wrote it down, numbers based on the flashes. A repeating pattern: 3 – 2 – 1 – 4 – 1 – 5 – 6 – 2 – 5 – 3 – 1."

Dr. Maddox took the notebook, eyebrows rising. "And you're sure this wasn't a mechanical glitch?"

"No way," Luke said. "It repeated, exactly the same. That's not random. It's a code."

"We showed it to Grandma," Alex added. "And she brought out this crazy metal thing, a Bazeries Cylinder. Said it was used for decoding messages back in the day."

"But you need a keyword," Luke said. "It must be a word with no repeating letters. We've been trying everything."

Alex turned his phone back to the photo. "And now we've got one. Trailbend. Ten letters. No repeats. And it's stamped right under the same symbol we just saw on the crate."

Dr. Maddox gave them a long, quiet look. "If someone's signaling from that lighthouse using an encrypted message, and you've found the key..."

Luke nodded. "Then we might be able to unlock the entire message."

Riley folded her arms, a small, impressed smile creeping onto her face. "And to think people underestimate kids."

Dr. Maddox set the notebook down carefully. "If this works, you two may have just uncovered something very serious."

Alex was already heading toward the door. "Then we'd better get back to Grandma's and try it."

Luke followed, grinning. "Time to turn those numbers into answers." Behind them, the waves rolled against the docks, as if the ocean itself was waiting to see what they'd discover next

Chapter 8 – Cracked, But Not Clear

The bikes screeched to a stop in Grandma Maggie's gravel driveway, tires spitting dust. Luke didn't even wait to take off his helmet; he was already up the porch steps and through the front door.

"Grandma!" he called. "We've got it, we think we found the key, it's Trailbend!"

She stepped out of the kitchen, a dish towel in one hand, flour smudged on her cheek. "Trailbend?" she asked, "How did you figure that out?"

Alex held up his phone, still displaying the photo. "It was stamped right on the crate. Ten letters, no repeats. It has to be the keyword."

Grandma gave a small, knowing smile and nodded toward the dining room. "Then let's not waste time."

They set the Bazeries Cylinder on the table, the wooden box already open beside it. Luke steadied the metal rod while carefully spinning the disks, one by one, until the top row lined up to spell the code word they found:

TRAILBEND

The letters snapped into place.

Luke unfolded the crumpled notebook page. "This is the full flash pattern," he said. "Every pause, every repeat."

He matched the sequence to the disks...

2, 1, 4, 4 / 3, 6 / 5, 2, 2, 1 / 6, 1 / 3, 4, 1, 1, 5...

copying each letter carefully from the row beneath. The room was silent except for the soft *click* of the turning rings. Bear watched from the windowsill, one eye half-open, like he was making sure Luke didn't mess up.

When Luke finished, he stared at the page. Then he read aloud.

"LOW TIDE HATCH / COORD LOCK / DROP POINT."

Alex leaned forward. "That's not a sentence."

"No," Luke said slowly. "It's instructions."

Maggie nodded. "Short. Exact. Whoever wrote this didn't want guesses, just action."

Alex frowned. "A hatch that only works at low tide...what could that be?"

"And 'coord lock' means the location is already decided," Luke added. "They didn't write the coordinates down because they didn't have to."

"A drop point," Maggie said quietly. "Somewhere to move something without being seen."

Alex swallowed. "The puffins."

Luke's stomach tightened. "They're planning a pickup."

Maggie looked toward the window, thoughtful. "If they're waiting for the lowest tides, that narrows things down. Around here, that usually happens in late June."

"How late?" Alex asked.

"Soon enough to matter," Maggie said.

Outside, the sun slid lower, turning the water gold, as if the day itself were trying to hide something before nightfall.

Alex yawned, rubbing his eyes. "I want to keep going, but my brain feels scrambled."

"That's enough for tonight," Maggie said gently, closing the cylinder and returning it to its box. "Sleep helps patterns settle. Tomorrow, we'll look at tide charts."

As they headed upstairs, Luke glanced back one last time at the message, its meaning clearer now than ever:

Low Tide Hatch

Coord Lock

Drop Point

Late June

Soon

Very soon.

"Good morning, boys!" Grandma Maggie's voice rang out like sunshine as Luke and Alex trudged into the kitchen, still rubbing sleep from their eyes.

On the table was one of her legendary breakfasts: a mountain of crispy bacon, thick slices of golden toast, a bowl of fresh blueberries and strawberries, and the star of the show...Dirty Potatoes. Luke's stomach growled at the sight. Chunks of leftover boiled potatoes, pan-fried in bacon fat until the edges were perfectly crisp, were tossed with crumbles of seasoned ground beef. The whole thing gave off a smell so rich it practically pulled them into their chairs.

"Whoa," Alex said, grabbing a plate. "You could solve world peace with this breakfast."

Grandma chuckled as she flipped the last strip of bacon onto a paper towel. "You'll need every bite. We're heading out with Red this morning, remember? Can't be chasing lobster traps on an empty stomach."

Luke scooped a pile of potatoes onto his plate. "Do you think some salty sea air will help us make sense of that weird message?"

"Maybe," Grandma said with a wink, pouring herself a cup of coffee. "Sometimes your brain just needs to be somewhere wild to put the pieces together. Or maybe you need to stop thinking and just let the answer find you."

Alex raised an eyebrow. "That sounds like something you learned from a spy movie."

She sipped her coffee without answering.

Luke grinned. "Or from actual experience."

Grandma just smiled mysteriously and handed each of them a slice of toast. "Eat up, detectives. You've got puzzles to solve and a boat to catch."

Luke and Alex boarded *The Salty Gale*, Captain Red's weathered boat, docked at the harbor's edge. The air was cool but promised warmth as the sun rose, turning the sky into a soft lavender and gold watercolor. The boys were buzzing with excitement as the boat set off, leaving the sleepy town behind. Grandma Maggie, dressed in layers with her windbreaker zipped up and a knit cap snug on her head, stood at the boat's edge, securing a cooler beneath a bench. The cool morning air off the water made her pull her jacket tighter, but she knew it would warm up soon as the sun rose higher. Uncle John stood at the stern with a thermos of coffee in hand, ready for the day ahead.

"I hope you boys are ready to catch some fish," Captain Red called from the bow. His voice was warm and deep, with a hint of laughter.

"We sure are," Luke grinned, practically bouncing with anticipation.

"Long as it doesn't involve bait that wriggles," Alex muttered, eyeing the slimy worms.

Uncle John chuckled. "You'll be fine, just follow Red's lead."

The boat cut through the still water, leaving the harbor behind. The sea stretched before them, gray and endless, dotted with lobster buoys and seabirds skimming the surface. The fog began to burn off as the sun climbed higher, revealing the rich blues and greens of the Maine coastline. The boys stood at the edge of the boat, eyes wide as they spotted distant islands and jagged cliffs in the rising light.

The boys dropped their lines near rocky outcroppings where kelp swayed. Luke cast his line with practiced ease. "Come on, Alex. You tied that fisherman's knot faster than I did yesterday. You've got this." The boys knew their knots well, bowlines, square knots, even the elusive monkey's fist. Part of their wilderness training back home, and something Uncle John had drilled into them on their last visit.

Minutes ticked by as they fished, the silence only broken by the occasional seagull's cry. Suddenly, Luke's rod jerked, and he grinned. "Got one!"

He reeled in with quick, fluid movements. A small mackerel splashed at the surface, thrashing against the water. With a quick flick, Luke unhooked it and released it back into the sea. "Not quite big enough for dinner, but a good start."

Alex laughed. "Maybe I'll have better luck." He cast his line again, watching it disappear into the water. But moments later, his line tangled with a mass of seaweed, and he pulled it up with a groan. "Well, that's not what I had in mind."

"Nothing like seaweed for lunch," Luke teased.

They spent another half hour fishing until Alex finally managed to catch a small mackerel, much to his relief. It wasn't the big fish he'd hoped for, but it was progress. "Looks like I'm catching lunch, too!" Alex said with a grin, holding up his fish.

Captain Red clapped him on the back. "Good job, kid. I'll make a real fisherman out of you yet."

After the fun of fishing, Captain Red called them over to the other side of the boat. "Time to check the traps." Red pulled up a heavy lobster trap dripping seawater, revealing two lobsters inside, one large and one small. "We measure them here," Red explained, showing them the gauge. "Too small, back they go. Too big, same deal. We only keep the just-right ones."

Luke leaned over, watching intently. "That makes sense. Keeps the population healthy."

As Red tossed the small lobster back into the water, Alex asked, "Is it hard to make a living fishing now?" His tone was serious, sensing the weight of Red's job.

"It's not what it used to be," Red said, wiping his hands on a rag. "Climate shifts, tighter rules, expensive gear all make it a rough way to make a living. But you get stubborn folks like me who just don't quit. There's no other way I'd want to live."

Just then, the sea erupted in a splash. "Whale!" Luke shouted, pointing toward the water.

A minke whale surfaced, its sleek back glistening in the sun before disappearing below the surface. The boys stared, wide-eyed with awe. "That was incredible," Alex whispered.

Grandma Maggie smiled warmly. "Nature's amazing!" she said, sipping her coffee. "Did you know that some whales can communicate over hundreds of miles? Humpback whales are interesting; they have these long, complex songs they sing to each other. And get this, scientists think they might have 'whale highways' across the oceans, with certain populations migrating on the same route every year. Imagine traveling that far without a map!"

"That's amazing," Luke said, still watching the spot where the whale had vanished.

After a while, Captain Red slowed the boat, cutting the engine to idle. The morning air was still, and the boat drifted toward a floating object in the distance.

"Captain Red, what's that?" Luke asked, squinting.

Red grabbed his binoculars and peered through them. "Looks like... an old crate. Might've broken loose in a storm."

They steered closer, and the crate appeared, bobbing just below the surface. It was waterlogged, the wood worn from the saltwater. As they got nearer, Alex reached down to pull a piece of wood that had broken off. A small piece of old paper was stuck to it. It looked like a piece of a map.

"That's odd," Luke said, holding the old scrap of paper. And look at this, there's a symbol here I don't recognize."

Red frowned, his fingers brushing the crate's worn edges. "I've seen a lot of crates, but nothing like this". But Alex and Luke had." I reckon it's been floating out in these waters for a while," Red said, starting the engine again.

Grandma Maggie leaned in, her eyes twinkling just a bit too know-ingly. "Well, well," she said, sipping her coffee without looking away from the symbol. "I'd say the sea just handed you boys, another piece of the puzzle."

Just as the boat reached the dock, Luke stood, clutching the small piece of map. "Thanks, Captain Red, for the amazing trip this morning. That was cool."

Grandma stretched and slid her coffee mug into her bag. "Well, that was a day worth remembering. But I need to get back home. I have an order to fill for a shop in town," said Grandma.

"Okay, Grandma," Alex replied. "We are going to head over to the research center and show Dr. Maddox what we found."

After unloading the lobsters, the boys retrieved their bikes and rode to the research center. The sun was high in the sky, and the town was starting to bustle with tourists.

When they arrived, they saw Riley working over a microscope in the lab. She looked up as the boys entered. "Whoa," she said, stopping short as they walked in with the crate. "Is that... another one?"

Luke nodded. "Pulled it straight out of the ocean. There was a map stuck to it.

Riley's eyes lit up. "That symbol again?"

Alex handed her the protected map sleeve. "It's there, near the top right."

"I'll get Dr. Maddox," she said, then paused. "Actually... this is weird timing, but I was going to mention something I found the other day."

Luke tilted his head. "What kind of something?"

"A tunnel could be an entrance to a cave," Riley said. "I found it while I was doing shoreline erosion research west of Sand Point. Super narrow entrance, totally invisible at high tide.

Alex blinked. "What could be in there?"

Riley nodded. "I didn't think much of it until now, but your light-house message. The entrance is near the North Cove. It might be what you are looking for."

Just then, Dr. Maddox stepped into the room, adjusting her glasses as she approached the table. "You're back already?" she asked, eyeing the crate and the damp sleeve in Luke's hands. "What did you bring me this time?"

Riley handed over the map fragment. "They recovered it this morning. It was stuck to this piece of crate floating off the coast."

Dr. Maddox carefully slid the fragment from the sleeve and laid it under a flat light. She studied it closely, turning it back and forth. "The edges are water-damaged," she said, "but the ink is surprisingly intact. This isn't centuries old, it's recent. The paper's fiber is commercially milled, probably from the last decade."

Luke leaned forward. "So, it's not some ancient pirate map?"

She smiled slightly. "No, but that might make it even more interesting. This looks like a functional map, designed for practical use, rather than decoration. Probably drawn by someone trying to keep things low-profile. If I didn't know what I was looking at, I might've thought it was a fisherman's sketch."

Alex pointed to the symbol. "But that's not something a random fisherman would draw."

"Exactly," Dr. Maddox said. "You've seen this symbol on the other piece of crate you found. If smugglers are marking their gear and locations with it, this map could be part of their navigation system. Something simple and analog on purpose."

"To avoid being tracked," Luke added, crossing his arms. "No GPS pings. No files to trace."

"Smart," Dr. Maddox said. "Low-tech means less risk of interception."

Alex's thoughts were racing. "Then this tunnel Riley found, it could be where they're storing something. Or moving birds through."

Riley nodded. "It lines up. The entrance disappears at high tide."

Alex's eyes widened. "That cave could be the drop point. We need to check it out."

Dr. Maddox nodded sharply. "Take photos of the interior. Look for airflow, tool marks, storage signs...anything that doesn't belong. But be careful. If this cave is active, whoever's using it won't want visitors."

Luke and Alex exchanged a look, pulses racing.

They had the map fragment.

They had the same symbol.

They had the decoded message.

And now... they had a place.

Whatever secrets were hiding in that cave? This time, they were ready to find them.

"But Dr. Maddox," Alex said suddenly, "shouldn't we... tell someone? Like the local police?"

Dr. Maddox nodded thoughtfully. "Absolutely. But not yet. We need hard facts and proof before making anything official. The wrong move could scare them off."

Luke swallowed. The stakes were growing. As they stepped out into the bright sunlight, their minds were racing with what they'd just learned.

The lighthouse signals.

The marked crates.

The cave hidden by the tides.

Something was coming together. They could feel it, but the final picture hadn't snapped into place just yet.

Chapter 9 – Where the Cliff Opened Up

As Luke and Alex walked back through town, the streets of Bar Harbor seemed to hold their breath in the evening air. The shops were closing, their lights flickering off one by one, and the smell of saltwater taffy from the candy store mixed with the faint scent of lobster from the restaurant down the street. The clink of glasses and the low hum of conversation spilled out from the local pubs, but the streets themselves were quieter now, the sounds of the town settling into the calm of dusk.

Luke's thoughts raced like a storm inside his head. He should have been excited. They were getting closer to solving the mystery, but instead, an uneasy feeling coiled in his gut, knotting tighter with every step. Something about all of this felt bigger than they could handle.

"Hey," Alex said, nudging him with his elbow as they passed a row of quiet, old houses with flower boxes hanging from the windows. "You okay?"

Luke hesitated, staring at the cobblestone streets underfoot. "I dunno. What if we mess this up? What if we get in too deep?"

Alex slowed down, his sneakers scuffing on the pavement as he thought. Alex shoved his hands in his pockets, looking at Luke with a raised eyebrow. "We stick together; we are a team. That's how we get through it," said Alex. "Like when we got lost on that mountain trail last fall."

Luke cracked a smile. "And you pulled out your backup compass, two protein bars, and a Mylar blanket like it was no big deal."

"Because I plan ahead. That's what I do," Alex said, nudging him again. "And you? You talk to people. You find clues."

"And Bear just sleeps through it all," Luke laughed.

A flash of movement caught Luke's eye as they passed the marina. Near the end of the dock, Ben stood with a man in a gray raincoat. They were speaking in low, quick voices. Ben looked agitated. The man handed him something small, then turned and disappeared behind a stack of lobster traps.

"Did you see that?" Luke whispered.

Alex nodded. "Yeah, that's weird. What's Ben doing here?"

They ducked behind a bait shack and watched Ben head off toward the research center, his posture tight, his shoulders hunched.

"I wonder what that was all about?" Alex said.

"Who knows," replied Luke. "One thing I do know is that I'm starving! Let's get back to Grandma's fast!"

As the evening settled over Bar Harbor, the boys and Grandma Maggie sat down for a hearty lobster dinner. The smell of fresh lobster, butter, and French fries filled the kitchen, and Bear, who had been dozing on the sofa, perked up at the sound of the food being served.

"Best meal of the day," Luke said with a grin, diving into his lobster.

Alex nodded, savoring the rich flavor. "I could eat this every day. But you know what I'm thinking about?"

"That tunnel Riley mentioned earlier?" Luke guessed, looking up from his plate.

Grandma Maggie paused, her fork halfway to her mouth. "A tunnel, huh? What did Riley have to say about this tunnel?"

Luke nodded, his eyes bright with urgency. "Riley found the cave down near the cove. It's hidden at high tide, but it lines up almost perfectly with Stormwatch Light. We think it might connect to the lighthouse signal. Maybe even to the message we decoded."

Alex jumped in, his voice low and serious. "The code said something about a hatch, a low tide, and coordinates. That cave could be part of a tunnel system or a drop point. It all fits."

Luke added, "And the crates we've seen? The markings match. The feather, the burn marks, it all points to something organized."

"And the puffins," Alex said. "That's what we think this whole thing is really about. Not just missing birds but trafficking."

He looked at Grandma, "We think they're using the cave to move them without being seen."

Grandma Maggie set down her utensils and folded her hands, "Well, if anyone can help you figure it out, it's John and me," she said with a knowing smile. "But before you run off, maybe we should think this through carefully. What exactly are you two planning?"

Luke glanced at Alex. "We were thinking of checking out the tunnel. But we don't know if it's safe or where to start looking."

Just as the conversation was taking a serious turn, Uncle John entered the room, carrying his thermos of coffee. "You boys still at it with this lighthouse business?" he asked, settling into a chair.

Luke and Alex filled him in on the new information they had learned from Riley about the tunnel, eager to hear what Uncle John might know.

"Well," Uncle John said, pouring himself a cup of coffee, "If you're headed that way, you need to know about the tides. Given the location Riley mentioned, it is probably only accessible at low tide, or you'll find yourself stuck. It's not the place you want to get trapped in."

Alex furrowed his brow. "How do we know when it's safe to go?"

Uncle John nodded sagely. "I've got some tide charts I can bring over tomorrow morning. They'll show you exactly when low tide is. Without them, you could show up at the wrong time, and the water will be up to your knees before you know it."

"Thanks, Uncle John," Luke said, feeling reassured. "So, we should wait until tomorrow, then?"

"Exactly," Uncle John replied. "It's important to know when the tides are right. We need to check the weather forecast too. Any large storms approaching can affect the tide. I'll help you plan it out. You won't want to get too close to the cliffs without proper timing."

The conversation drifted to other matters, but the mystery of the tunnel and the lighthouse still hung in the air. The boys knew that tomorrow, with the tide chart in hand, they would be one step closer to discovering what was really going on.

Grandma Maggie rose as the meal wound down and started clearing the table. "You boys be careful," she warned. "I understand your concern for the puffins, but I am concerned about your safety." Luke and

Alex exchanged glances, both knowing that Grandma was right. Their wilderness training taught them to always have a plan and a backup plan, and to know when things were too dangerous.

It was a beautiful morning in Bar Harbor as Luke and Alex sat at Grandma Maggie's kitchen table, their eyes scanning the tide chart Uncle John had spread before them. "Understanding tides is key," Uncle John said, running his finger along the lines on the chart. "The moon has a powerful gravitational pull on the sea, making the water rise and fall. See these peaks here?" He pointed to the chart, where the lines shot upward. "Those are high tides. And the dips..." he gestured to the troughs that followed..."show the low tides." The moon's gravity causes this, pulling on the water as if guided by a giant invisible hand."

Alex leaned in, trying to follow the lines. "So, when the moon's closer, the tides get bigger?"

Exactly," Uncle John said. "The closer the moon is to Earth, the stronger its pull. That's when the tides are highest. We must be there during low tide for our hike, or the entrance to the cave will be submerged, and we won't be able to explore it."

Alex absorbed the information, nodding. "Our hike?" Alex questioned.

"Yes," said Uncle John. " I know you boys are skilled and resourceful explorers, but sometimes it's good to have an adult around just in case."

"Actually, that sounds great, Uncle John," Luke responded. "You can never be too careful. So, according to this, the low tide is at 10:15 AM. If we head out now, we'll have plenty of time to check the tunnel before the water returns."

Grandma Maggie entered the room, handing each boy a packed lunch and a water bottle. "Remember," she said with a wink, "the ocean is unpredictable. Keep your wits about you and don't dawdle."

"Thanks, Grandma," Luke said, slipping the provisions into his backpack.

With their gear packed and the tide timing set, the boys and Uncle John set off for the coast. The trail wound through a thick forest of spruce and fir, the scent of pine needles filling the air. Alex took the lead, his gaze fixed on the compass, ensuring they stayed on track toward the Atlantic Ocean.

After bushwacking their way through a thick grove of evergreen trees, they emerged and were greeted by a stunning view of the Atlantic Ocean. The tide had receded, exposing a rocky shore lined with tide pools.

"Check this out!" Luke shouted, dropping to his knees next to a small pool. Inside, sea anemones danced in the current, their tentacles flashing every rainbow color. A starfish clung to a nearby rock, its five arms spread wide, while barnacles coated the stones like little white shells.

Alex crouched next to him, eyes wide in wonder. "Tide pools are like little underwater worlds," he said. "When the tide's out, they trap all these creatures, making them like their own little ecosystems. The creatures had adapted to survive underwater and exposed to the air." They knelt, watching tiny crabs scuttling among the rocks and small fish darting through the water.

"These guys are tough little survivors," Luke mused. "They thrive in two completely different worlds. That's really amazing."

They continued along the shore, making their way towards the towering cliffs Riley had mentioned. The massive rock formations were layered in bands, each telling a story of geological history.

"Riley explained this to me. I like her enthusiasm for geology," Alex said, pointing to the distinct layers in the cliff face. "These layers are sedimentary rock, formed over millions of years. But see that dark section? That's igneous rock, created from cooled lava. And over there, where the rock is twisted and folded—that's metamorphic rock, which has been transformed by intense heat and pressure."

Luke ran his hand over the rough surface of the rock. "I think it's amazing how the Earth can tell its own story if you learn how to read it."

As they made their way along the cliffs, they watched their footing. Uncle John said, "Be careful, especially on the wet rocks; they can be very slippery. And do your best not to disturb the habitat."

Alex, Luke, and Uncle John finally reached the secluded cove. There, seals lounging on the rocks, their sleek bodies glistening, and a bald eagle soared overhead, its sharp eyes scanning the waters below for an easy fish to catch.

"It's like something out of a nature documentary on television," Luke whispered, watching in amazement.

They continued on, their excitement building with each step. As they neared the base of the cliff, Luke noticed a series of fresh boot prints leading toward a narrow fissure in the rock. "These prints are recent," he observed. "And they're heading straight for that crack in the rock."

They approached cautiously, discovering the entrance to the hidden tunnel. The mouth of the tunnel was just wide enough for them to slip through.

"Here it is," Alex said, his voice tinged with excitement.

Luke glanced at his watch. "We only have about thirty minutes before the tide comes back in. Let's move quickly."

Inside, the tunnel was cold and damp. The air was thick with the scent of saltwater and something else, fish. Their flashlights illuminated the walls, and when something caught their eye, it was a wooden crate wedged between two rocks. The crate had the same, now familiar symbol burned into it.

Alex knelt down and picked up a small metal band wedged into the rocks nearby. He turned it over and inspected the engraving, which was a series of numbers. "This looks like a bird band," Alex said, his voice low. "The kind that researchers will use to track puffins.

"Luke's eyes widened. "This is a vital clue!"

The boys looked at each other in stunned silence, unable to believe what they had just found. Alex stuffed the band into his backpack, his mind racing with questions.

"We've gotta tell Dr. Maddox about this," Alex said, his voice urgent. "We can't waste any more time here. The tide's coming in fast."

Luke nodded, glancing over his shoulder one last time. "Agreed, let's get out of here." They quickly gathered their things, the weight of their discovery sinking in. They were now convinced that Puffins were being poached! Now the questions were: who was involved, and how could they stop it?

As they hurried back toward the shore, the air grew colder. The tunnel's damp, barnacle-covered walls gave way to the salty breeze of the open ocean. As they clambered over the rocks, Luke noticed something strange. A figure, high above on the cliff, stood watching them.

"Alex, look!" Luke whispered, pointing. Alex squinted toward the figure. It was too far away to make out any details, but the posture was unmistakable; someone was watching. A shiver ran down Luke's spine. "We need to be careful."

"Let's head back," Alex said, his voice low. "We'll tell Dr. Maddox what we found."

With the weight of their discovery on their shoulders, they made their way back home, knowing they were getting closer to the truth. But with every step, the mystery deepened, and the feeling that they were being watched only grew stronger.

The boys recounted their adventure with Grandma Maggie, telling her about the hidden tunnel and the bird band. Grandma Maggie listened intently, her expression a mix of worry and pride.

"You did the right thing, paying close attention to the tides and coming back right away," she said, her voice steady but serious. "But this is bigger than we thought. We've got to be careful from here on out."

Just then, Uncle John, who'd been listening from the doorway, stepped into the room. "I'll check in with some old friends of mine," he said quietly. "Keep things low-key for now. I think you boys should stay close to home for now." The boys nodded. Their wilderness training taught them when to reassess a situation and make a new plan.

Chapter 10 – Shadows Closing In

The morning sun bathed Bar Harbor in a golden light. Still, inside the Bar Harbor Wildlife Research Center, the air felt heavy with an underlying tension. Dr. Evelyn Maddox had already been out on the water that morning, her paddleboard cutting through the calm sea as the sun rose. She had enjoyed the quiet, the peaceful rhythm of the waves, a moment of mindfulness before the day's work began.

Evelyn had spent her whole life immersed in wildlife research and conservation. From her earliest days, she had worked as a volunteer at a local nature reserve, helping to clean up beaches and monitor bird nests, learning the value of preserving the natural world at a young age. Over the years, she built a career by traveling the globe and working in various conservation programs. Still, Bar Harbor was where she had settled. With its rugged coastlines and pristine wilderness, this place was unlike anywhere else she had ever been, and where she felt most at home.

But now, back at her desk, a feeling of unease settled over her. Her brow furrowed in concentration as she sifted through the reports on puffin migration patterns. The recent anomalies, like disrupted signals and lower-than-normal bird counts, nagged at her, like a puzzle she couldn't quite solve. Poaching was a huge issue for wildlife and something she had always known existed, but it had never touched her directly. She had read about it, heard the stories, but never encountered it firsthand. Now, as the data didn't add up and the birds seemed to vanish without a trace, she couldn't shake the nagging feeling that there was something more than natural reasons for what was happening.

A sharp knock interrupted her thoughts.

Before she could respond, the door opened, and Ben, her research assistant, stepped into her office. His usual easygoing demeanor was overshadowed by a furrowed brow and restless energy.

"Morning, Dr. Maddox," Ben greeted, avoiding direct eye contact. "I compiled the latest data on the puffin colonies. Thought you'd want to review it."

She accepted the folder, noting the slight tremor in his hand. "Thank you, Ben. Is everything alright? You seem... unsettled."

He hesitated, then forced a smile that didn't reach his eyes. "Just a bit tired. Long night analyzing data."

Before Dr. Maddox could probe further, the shrill ring of her office phone cut through the tension. She picked up, and the familiar, soothing voice of Grandma Maggie filled the room.

"Evelyn, dear, I hope I'm not catching you at a bad time," Maggie began.

"Not at all," Dr. Maddox replied, glancing at Ben, who had taken a keen interest in the conversation.

"The boys have come across some information they believe is pertinent to your research," Grandma continued. "Would you be able to stop by this afternoon for tea? They'd like to share their findings with you."

Dr. Maddox's curiosity piqued. "Of course. I'll be there around three."

As she hung up, she noticed Ben's posture stiffen. His eyes darted away, and he busied himself with the papers on her desk.

"Everything okay, Ben?" she inquired, her tone gentle but probing.

He forced another smile. "Yeah, just remembered I have some errands to run. If you'll excuse me." Ben exited without waiting for a response, leaving Dr. Maddox with a lingering sense of unease.

Dr. Maddox arrived at Grandma Maggie's beautiful cottage at precisely three o'clock. The aroma of freshly baked scones and brewing tea welcomed her as she stepped inside.

Luke and Alex sat at the kitchen table, their faces a mix of excitement and apprehension. Bear lounged at their feet, occasionally thumping his tail against the wooden floor.

"Dr. Maddox, thank you for coming," Luke began, his voice steady but tinged with urgency.

"We found something when we explored the cave," Alex added, pulling out the puffin band and the photographs they had taken of the crate inside the sea cave.

Dr. Maddox examined the items, her brow furrowing deeper with each passing moment. "This band belongs to one of our missing puffins," she confirmed. "And these markings on the crate are not from any official research equipment. It's the same markings that we saw on the two pieces of crate you found earlier."

Grandma Maggie poured tea for everyone, her eyes betraying a storm of thoughts. "There's more," she said softly. "The boys mentioned seeing a figure watching them from the lighthouse."

Dr. Maddox's grip tightened around the teacup. "This aligns with some concerns I've had at the research center. Ben has been acting... off lately. Distracted, evasive. And he overheard our conversation this morning."

Luke exchanged a glance with Alex. "Do you think Ben could be involved in the puffin disappearances?"

Dr. Maddox sighed, the weight of responsibility pressing heavily upon her. "I hate to think so and don't want to jump to conclusions without evidence. But his recent behavior raises questions."

Alex leaned forward. "We've also heard that Eli has been seen out by the lighthouse. Do you think he could be involved?"

Dr. Maddox set her cup down, her resolve hardening her features. "We need to approach this methodically. I'll discreetly look into Ben's activities at the center. In the meantime, it's best if you boys stay close to home. Let Uncle John, your Grandma, and me handle the investigation for now."

Luke and Alex nodded, understanding the gravity of the situation. Yet, the spark of adventure and the drive to uncover the truth burned brightly within them.

As the sun dipped below the horizon, painting the sky with shades of orange and pink, Dr. Evelyn Maddox locked up the Bar Harbor Wildlife Research Center. The last rays of light stretched across the town, casting long shadows along the streets. But as she stood there, the weight of the day's discoveries pressing on her mind, she couldn't shake the uneasy feeling that someone, or something was watching her.

The chill in the evening air seemed to echo that strange sense of being followed, making the quiet town feel much more mysterious than usual. She slipped her keys into her bag and turned...

"Dr. Maddox."

She startled.

Ben stood a few feet away, half in shadow. His hair was damp with sweat, his eyes wild like he hadn't slept in days.

"Ben?" she said gently. "What are you doing here so late?"

He wiped his forehead with the sleeve of his hoodie. "I—I needed to talk to you. Please. Just a minute."

"Of course," she said, concern rising. "What's wrong?"

His words tumbled out too fast. "I'm sorry. I'm so sorry. I didn't mean for any of this to happen. I swear. I tried to stop it."

Dr. Maddox stepped closer. "Stop what, Ben?"

He laughed weakly, hands shaking. "Everything. All of it. I thought I could fix it before you noticed. Before anyone got hurt."

"Ben," she said, calm but firm, "you're not making sense. Talk to me."

Tears welled in his eyes. "They're watching me. If I mess up, if I talk, it's over. My future. My family. Everything."

"Who's watching you?" she asked.

He shook his head wildly. "I can't say. You don't understand. You don't know what he's like."

Dr. Maddox reached out, touching his arm. "Ben, look at me. Whatever you did, we can deal with it together. You're not alone."

That was when something inside him snapped. "I am alone!" he shouted, pulling away. His breathing came in ragged gasps. "You can't help me! Nobody can!"

"Ben—"

"I'm sorry," he whispered suddenly. "I really am."

Before she could react, he grabbed her wrist.

"What are you doing?" she gasped.

Riley had just wrapped up hours of studying when she turned into the quiet parking lot behind the research center, her backpack heavy with books and her mind still buzzing with facts and formulas. She was already thinking about leftover pizza for dinner and a hot shower when she heard the raised voices of Ben and Dr. Maddox cutting through the evening air.

Riley's stomach dropped. Something was wrong. Very wrong. "Ben?" she called out. "What are you doing?"

He spun toward her, eyes wide and wild, like a cornered animal. For a second, Riley thought he might stop. Apologize. Walk away.

Instead, his grip tightened on Dr. Maddox's arm.

"Don't," Dr. Maddox warned. "This isn't the answer."

Ben didn't listen. He dragged her toward a car idling in the shadows. Dr. Maddox struggled, her shoes scraping against the pavement.

"Ben, let go!" Riley shouted, sprinting forward. But it was too late.

Ben shoved Dr. Maddox into the passenger seat and slammed the door so hard the windows rattled. He hesitated for half a second, his chest heaving, eyes flicking to Riley.

"I'm sorry," he mouthed.

Then he jumped into the driver's seat, turned the key, and sped off into the night.

Riley's heart slammed against her ribs, her thoughts tumbling over each other. *What is happening? Why is he doing this?* She didn't stop to think. She couldn't. Dr. Maddox needed help now.

Riley broke into a sprint, backpack bouncing against her shoulders as she chased after the car. Her sneakers slapped against the pavement, her lungs burning as she pushed herself harder.

"Stop!" she shouted, though she knew he couldn't hear her.

The car's taillights glowed for a second, then vanished around the corner. Riley slowed, bending over with her hands on her knees, gasping for breath. Fear twisted in her stomach. She was too late. But she wasn't giving up.

Spinning on her heel, Riley took off again, this time toward Grandma Maggie's house. The streets were quiet, porch lights flickering on as evening settled in, but Riley barely noticed. Her mind raced faster than her feet. *Ben took her. He forced her. Dr. Maddox is in trouble.*

She burst through Maggie's front door without knocking, nearly tripping over the welcome mat. "Grandma! Uncle John!" she cried, voice shaking. "Something's happened to Dr. Maddox!"

Chapter 11 – Hostage at Stormwatch Light

Grandma Maggie, Uncle John, and the boys were in the middle of a heated game of gin rummy when Riley burst through the front door, breathless and wide-eyed.

Maggie jumped up from her chair and Uncle John was on his feet instantly.

"Slow down, Riley," Maggie said gently. "You're safe here. Tell us what has happened."

Riley sucked in air, hands trembling. "Ben…he grabbed Dr. Maddox. He shoved her into a car and drove off. I tried to stop him. I really did." Riley swallowed hard. Fear still clawed at her chest, but beneath it burned something stronger. Determination.

Maggie straightened, eyes sharp. "Riley, breathe. Then start from the beginning. Tell us exactly what happened."

Riley took a shaky breath and explained everything. How she had heard loud voices and realized that it was Ben and Dr. Maddox quarreling in the parking lot. His frantic apology. The way he grabbed Dr. Maddox and shoved her into the car, and how the engine roared as he sped away.

When she finished, silence filled the room.

Uncle John's jaw tightened. "If Ben took her against her will, she could be in real danger," he said, his voice low and controlled. "We can't waste any time."

Luke and Alex locked eyes across the table. It was the look they'd shared a hundred times before: right before climbing a tree that looked too tall, right before sneaking out to investigate a strange noise. The look that meant we've got this. Together.

"We have to help her," Alex said, his voice tight. "We can't just sit here and wait for someone else to fix this. I bet no one else even knows she's missing yet?"

Luke nodded. "And I think I know where he went. The lighthouse. That figure we saw the other night? It has to have been Ben. It all makes sense now."

Riley's eyes widened. "You really think so?"

"Yeah," Luke said. "He was hanging around there like he didn't want to be seen. We just didn't put it together."

Maggie folded her arms, her expression serious. "I believe you're right. That place is too remote for coincidences."

Uncle John stepped closer to the table. "Stormwatch Light is out of the way. No tourists. No witnesses. If someone wanted privacy…"

"That's where they'd go," Alex finished.

Maggie nodded. "But listen to me. We don't charge in like a pack of wild seals. We need to use our heads and make a plan."

Luke bounced anxiously on his toes. "So what's the plan?"

"The plan," Maggie said, "is to move quietly. We watch first. We don't let them see us coming."

Riley hugged her arms around herself. "What if he hurts her?"

Maggie's voice softened. "We're not going to let that happen."

Alex clenched his fists. "Not if we can stop it."

Maggie slipped on her jacket and slung her pack over one shoulder in a single, fluid motion. Luke blinked. He had never noticed just how nimble she was. For the first time that night, Luke felt like he might be in over his head. The thought made his stomach tighten, but he didn't say anything.

Under the cover of darkness, the group moved carefully toward the lighthouse. The narrow path hugged the cliff, and every step felt risky. Slick rocks gleamed in the moonlight, and the wind tugged at their jackets like invisible hands trying to pull them off balance.

Riley walked a little behind the others, focused on her footing. Suddenly, her boot slipped on a patch of wet stone. "Ow!" she cried, stumbling forward.

Luke spun around. "Riley!"

Alex caught her elbow just before she went down. "Easy, easy," he said. "Sit, don't move."

Riley sank onto a rock, her face pale. "I think I twisted my ankle," she said, biting her lip. "It hurts… a lot."

Luke crouched beside her. "Can you move it?"

She tried and winced. "Not really."

Alex frowned, gently inspecting it. "It's already swelling. That's not great."

Luke pulled the orange bandana from his pocket. "Okay, compression," he said, trying to sound calm even though his hands were shaking. "This should help a little."

He wrapped it snugly around her ankle. Riley let out a shaky breath. "Thanks."

Alex slid a flat stone under her foot. "Elevate it. It'll slow the swelling."

Riley leaned back against the rock, eyes glistening. "I'm so sorry," she said. "I don't want to slow you down."

"You're not," Luke said quickly. "This isn't your fault."

She looked up at them. "You have to go. Dr. Maddox needs you. I'll be okay here."

Luke hesitated. "Are you sure?"

Riley nodded, forcing a small smile. "Positive."

Uncle John knelt beside her and pulled a flashlight from his pocket. "If anything goes wrong, you signal with this."

"How?" Riley asked.

"Three short flashes, three long, three short," he explained. "SOS.

Riley gripped the flashlight. "I won't mess it up."

John met her eyes. "I know you won't. You're brave, Riley. Braver than you think."

Maggie squeezed her shoulder. "Stay hidden. If anyone comes near, don't make a sound."

"I will," Riley promised.

Luke hesitated one last second. "We'll be back. I swear."

"I know," Riley said. "Go."

They stood, hearts pounding, then turned toward the looming lighthouse. Riley watched them disappear into the darkness, clutching the flashlight like it was her lifeline.

The remaining group approached the lighthouse cautiously. Its towering silhouette loomed against the night sky, and the once-bright beacon, meant to provide a safe harbor, was now dark. Uncle John raised his finger to his lips, signaling silence as they entered through a side door that creaked ominously.

They crept through the narrow, dusty corridors, moving so quietly that even their breathing felt too loud. Cobwebs brushed against their faces and arms, making Luke shiver as he fought the urge to swat them away. The air smelled stale, like old paper and forgotten rooms, and every step sent tiny clouds of dust drifting into the beam of Alex's flashlight.

Somewhere in the darkness, water dripped slowly—drip... drip... drip—echoing through the stone halls like a warning.

From a distant room, low voices floated toward them, muffled but tense. The words were impossible to make out, but the urgency in them made Alex's stomach twist.

Grandma Maggie leaned in, her whisper barely a breath against Luke's ear. "That must be them," she said.

The voices grew closer, and the group flattened themselves against the wall, hearts pounding, knowing one careless move could give them away.

They edged closer, pressing their faces to a narrow crack in the door. Inside, Dr. Maddox sat bound to a wooden chair, rope biting into her wrists. Dust floated in the beam of moonlight spilling through a shattered window, but her posture was straight, her chin lifted in unbroken defiance.

Ben paced in front of her, hands clenched into fists, his footsteps sharp and restless. "You shouldn't have meddled," he snapped. "Now look where it's gotten you."

Dr. Maddox met his glare without flinching. "It's not too late, Ben. You can still make this right."

He shook his head, a bitter edge creeping into his voice. "You don't understand. I'm in too deep."

Outside the door, Uncle John turned to the group, whispering urgently, "We need a distraction."

Luke's fingers brushed the small mirror in his pocket. His eyes sparked. "I've got one." He eased it out and carefully angled it toward the broken window, catching a thin blade of moonlight. He waited, heart hammering, for the perfect moment.

Inside, Dr. Maddox tugged at the ropes. "Ben, you didn't have to do any of this. If something was wrong, you could've come to me. I would've helped you."

Ben stopped pacing, his voice cracking. "You don't get it. I didn't have a choice."

"There's always a choice," she said firmly. "What we decide defines who we are. You chose to lie. To betray your team. But it doesn't have to end this way."

His shoulders sagged. "They threatened me. Said they'd destroy my future—my reputation. I was only supposed to give them the tag numbers. That's it."

"And then?" she pressed. "Help them move live birds? Erase tracking data? What happens to the puffins after they're smuggled out?"

Ben swallowed hard. "I know."

"You can still take responsibility," she said softly. "But first you need to let me go."

Uncle John's voice cut through the tension. "Now, Luke."

Luke tilted the mirror. A sudden flash of moonlight burst across the room, blinding Ben and startling him. He cried out, stumbling back as thunder boomed overhead.

At the same instant, the door flew open. Uncle John stormed in, flashlight blazing. Luke and Alex followed close behind. Grandma Maggie stepped in last, calm and steady, her eyes sharp as sea glass.

"Step away from her, Ben," Uncle John growled.

Ben backed toward the wall, panic flooding his face. "You don't understand, if they find out I talked..."

Before he could finish, a heavy clunk echoed behind them. The door slammed shut. They were trapped.

Somewhere outside, footsteps hurried away.

Luke spun around. "They locked us in."

Uncle John tested the handle, but it wouldn't budge. "Looks like your friends want to keep us quiet."

Luke dropped to one knee and pulled out his multi-tool, flipping it open with a quiet click. Alex knelt beside him, shining his flashlight low so the beam wouldn't spill under the door.

"Try the hinge first," Alex whispered. "If we can loosen it..."

Luke nodded. His hands moved quickly but carefully, slipping the flat edge into the narrow gap. The metal scraped softly as he worked. "Almost... got it..." Luke muttered.

Behind them, Uncle John hurried to Dr. Maddox. He sliced through the rope with his pocket knife, and it fell away from her wrists. She gasped in relief, rubbing the red marks.

"Are you okay?" he asked.

"I will be," she said. "But Ben, he's not a bad person. He just made bad choices."

Ben sank onto a crate, burying his face in his hands. "It started last year," he said quietly. "Trevor Langly was my instructor. Everyone respected him. He had all the power."

"What happened?" Maggie asked gently.

Ben swallowed. "I messed up. Cheated on a test. Once. Then I skipped a safety protocol on a field assignment. He caught me. Said he'd report me, ruin my career before it even started."

Dr. Maddox shook her head. "That's abuse of power, Ben. He should've helped you learn from your mistakes, not threaten you."

Ben's voice trembled. "He kept holding it over me. Every time I tried to pull away, he'd remind me. Said I owed him. That if I didn't help with the tracking numbers, he'd expose me."

Uncle John frowned. "That's blackmail."

"I know," Ben said. "But I was scared. He made me feel trapped."

Maggie stepped closer, her voice firm but kind. "When someone has power over you and uses it to control you, that's wrong. No matter what you did before."

Dr. Maddox nodded. "The right thing to do is tell someone you trust. A supervisor. Authorities. Keeping quiet only lets them keep hurting people."

Ben looked up, eyes glassy. "I didn't think anyone would believe me."

Across the room—"Got it!" Luke whispered.

The old rusty hinge loosened. Alex wedged the tool in and pushed. The wood creaked. "Together," Alex said.

They shoved, slow and steady, until the hinge finally popped with a dull crack. The door swung open.

Luke grinned. "Team effort."

Uncle John grabbed his bag. "Time to move. We don't know how long we have."

Ben stood, shoulders straighter than before. "I'll tell you everything about Trevor. Everything."

Dr. Maddox placed a hand on his arm. "That's the first right choice you've made tonight."

They hurried through the doorway and onto the steps of the lighthouse and then froze.

Voices drifted through the fog, low and close. Heavy boots thudded against the dock boards, each step slow and deliberate.

Maggie's eyes narrowed. "Looks like the night isn't over yet."

Outside, the rocky clearing at the base of the lighthouse glimmered with damp stone and drifting mist. And they weren't alone.

Three figures materialized from the fog. Men in dark rain gear. Boots crunching over gravel. Flashlights sliced pale tunnels through the haze. Radios murmuring at their shoulders.

"Well, well," the tallest one drawled as he stepped forward. "Look what we've got here. The little detectives... and their babysitters." His grin was thin and dangerous.

Behind him, the other two spread out, blocking every escape.

Grandma Maggie stopped short. Her jaw tightened. "Trevor Langley."

He gave a short, humorless laugh. "Still sharp as ever, Maggie. I was wondering if you'd recognize me."

Luke looked between them. "You know this guy?"

"I do," Maggie said plainly. "Trevor used to work maritime enforcement. Knows these waters. Knows the rules, too. Which makes it worse that he's breaking them."

Langley shrugged. "Morals don't pay the bills, Maggie."

"Laws were written to protect what can't protect itself," Maggie said. "You let money be more important than that."

Before anyone could react, another man came out from behind the lighthouse. He carried a wooden crate with the words LIVE CARGO stamped across the side.

Maggie's eyes flashed. "So this is what it's really about," she said. "You are really selling live puffins to the highest bidder?"

Trevor turned toward her, his jaw tight. "You should have stayed out of it, Maggie."

She stepped closer. "Stayed out of what? You threatening a student? Blackmailing him into doing your dirty work?"

His face darkened. "Ben made his own choices."

"You made those choices for him," Maggie shot back. "You knew he was scared. You used your power to trap him."

Trevor scoffed. "You don't understand what it's like out here. People are desperate. There aren't many chances to get ahead."

"So you decided to take advantage of that?" Maggie said. "You decided to profit off stolen wildlife and ruined futures?"

He hesitated, just for a moment. "I did what I had to do."

"No," Maggie said firmly. "You did what was easiest. There's a difference."

Trevor's voice rose. "You think you're better than me?"

"I think you used to be better," Maggie replied. "And that's what makes this so hard to watch."

The man with the crate cleared his throat. "Boss, we gotta move."

Trevor didn't look away from Maggie. "This is on you and those boys," he said. "They poked around where they didn't belong, and you didn't stop them."

Maggie stood her ground. "No, Trevor. This is on you. Every bit of it."

He finally turned away. "Get them on the boat," he snapped. "Now."

Fog curled tighter around their feet as waves crashed below. Luke felt the moment shift, like a door slamming shut. They hadn't just uncovered the truth. They had stepped straight into the storm.

They were herded at flashlight-point toward a small dock where a sleek, unmarked boat waited. Luke and Alex exchanged anxious glances. The puffin crates were already on board, lined in straw, with soft chirping sounds coming from inside.

Ben glanced at the boys. "You don't know what they're capable of."

"No," Alex said coldly. "But I think you do."

They were shoved aboard. Dr. Maddox sat beside Luke, her wrists red from the ropes.

One of the smugglers threw the engine into gear, and the boat roared to life. Cold wind whipped across the deck as the shoreline shrank behind them.

Grandma Maggie kept her eyes locked on Langley. "So this is who you've become, Trevor. I never thought you'd sink this low."

He sneered. "You and John always acted like you were better than the rest of us."

Uncle John gave a slow shake of his head. "No. We just chose not to cross lines we couldn't uncross. That's the difference."

Trevor's face darkened. "You don't get to judge me."

"I'm not judging," John said quietly. "I'm telling you the truth."

That did it.

Trevor surged forward, shoving John hard in the chest. The two men collided, grappling near the edge of the boat. Their boots scraped on the wet deck as they struggled for balance.

"John!" Maggie shouted, rushing toward them.

Luke stepped forward without thinking. "Uncle John, watch out!"

Trevor twisted suddenly, throwing his elbow back. It clipped Luke's shoulder. Luke staggered, his foot catching on the corner of a crate. For a split second, his arms pinwheeled as he tried to steady himself.

"Luke!" Alex screamed.

Luke's eyes widened in shock. The world tipped. The railing vanished beneath him. Then he was gone. Splash.

The sound hit Alex like a punch to the chest. "No—no—no!" Alex ran to the edge, his heart pounding so hard it hurt. He dropped to his knees, scanning the dark water. "Luke! LUKE!"

His cousin. His best friend. His hiking partner. Gone.

The boat surged forward, engine roaring, pulling them farther away with every second.

Maggie rushed to the rail, gripping it with white knuckles. "Oh no... Luke..." Her voice broke, but her eyes stayed fierce, searching the black waves.

Uncle John tore free and sprinted forward. "Luke! Hold on!" he shouted into the night. But there was only darkness and churning water.

Alex felt a sick, helpless knot tighten in his chest. The cold fear crawled up his spine as he realized they were moving farther and farther away from Luke.

Chapter 12 – A Test Of Courage

Water slammed over Luke's head like a trapdoor snapping shut, swallowing him in freezing darkness. The shock of the Atlantic crushed the air from his lungs, and for one terrifying moment, he couldn't move at all. Panic clawed at his chest, but he forced himself to kick, fighting against the heavy drag of his soaked clothes. At last, he burst to the surface with a ragged gasp.

Float, he told himself, Uncle John's voice steady in his mind. *Don't panic. Just float.*

The cold felt like a thousand needles stabbing his skin, but Luke forced himself onto his back, spreading his arms and legs wide. The salty waves lifted and dropped him like a leaf, and he stared up at the black sky, breathing slowly through chattering teeth. *I'm okay. Stay calm. Conserve energy.*

His mind flashed back to the boat, Trevor shoving Uncle John, boots slipping on the slick deck. Luke had stepped forward without thinking, trying to help. Then an elbow had clipped his shoulder. His foot caught on a crate. The shove hadn't been meant for him. But he had paid the price.

Now the boat was speeding away, its engine fading into the fog. Fear twisted in his stomach as thoughts of Alex, Grandma Maggie, his parents, Jake, and even Bear rushed through his mind. *I can't disappear like this.*

A sharp cramp seized his leg, and Luke sucked in a breath. He tried to kick, but the strength wasn't there anymore. His arms felt like lead.

Hold on, he told himself. *Just a little longer.*

Riley crouched on the jagged rocks near the lighthouse, her ankle pulsing with pain. She had tried to climb down after the others, but one wrong step sent lightning shooting up her leg, and she nearly lost her balance.

The tide was creeping higher. Cold water splashed closer to her shoes, and fear crawled up her spine as she realized the waves were cutting off her way back. She couldn't stay. But she couldn't climb, either.

Think, Riley. You've got to think. Then she grabbed her flashlight and waved it wildly out to sea, sweeping the beam through the fog in fast, sharp arcs.

Her arm burned. She didn't stop. Then she heard it. A low hum. An engine.

Hope burst through her chest as a sturdy boat emerged from the mist, riding the waves as if it knew them by heart. At the helm stood Eli, his weathered face locked in focus.

"Riley!" he shouted. "Hang on!" He steered closer than anyone else would have dared and tossed her a rope. "Wrap it around yourself tight!"

Her fingers were numb from the cold, but she looped the rope around her waist and pulled it snug. When she raised her arm, Eli braced himself and hauled.

A wave knocked her sideways, and she slipped, but the rope held. Eli pulled again, muscles straining. With one final tug, he dragged her safely aboard. Riley collapsed, shaking as he wrapped a thick blanket around her shoulders.

"You're safe now," he said softly. "Maggie would never forgive me if I let anything happen to you."

Riley blinked. "You know Grandma Maggie?"

Eli nodded. "Years ago, she pulled me out of a winter storm when my motor died. Coldest night of my life. Guess I owe her."

Tears filled Riley's eyes. "They took them. Alex, Grandma, Uncle John, Dr. Maddox... and Luke fell off the boat into the water. I could hear the screams from the boat."

Eli's jaw tightened. "Hold on." He shoved the throttle forward, and the boat surged into the dark.

Luke's arms were numb now. Every wave felt heavier than the last, and his voice barely worked when he tried to shout. "Help!" he croaked, but the fog swallowed the sound.

His legs cramped again, sharp pain twisting through his calves. Panic surged, but he forced it down. *Slow breaths. You've got this.*

Then he heard it. The hum of an engine. A beam of light cut through the fog. Relief crashed over him so hard his eyes burned.

"LUKE!" Riley's voice carried faintly over the wind.

He summoned all the energy he had left and lifted his stiff arms and waved weakly.

Moments later, Eli maneuvered alongside him. Strong hands grabbed his jacket and hauled him aboard. Luke collapsed onto the deck, coughing up seawater and shaking uncontrollably. "You okay, kid?" Eli asked, wrapping him in a blanket.

Luke nodded, teeth chattering. "They've got my family. We have to go after them."

Eli didn't hesitate. "Already on it."

On the smugglers' boat, tension crackled in the salty air. Maggie sat straight-backed, her eyes never leaving Trevor.

"So this is who you've become," she said quietly.

Trevor scoffed. "Careful."

"You trapped Ben," Maggie said. "Used your power to blackmail him."

Trevor glanced toward Ben, who stood frozen near the railing. His jaw tightened. "He made mistakes."

"And you punished him instead of helping him," Maggie shot back. "That's not leadership. That's cruelty."

Dr. Maddox leaned forward. "Smuggling endangered animals is a federal crime, Trevor. You're ruining lives."

"You have no idea what I'll lose if this falls apart!" he snapped, panic creeping into his voice.

Maggie noticed it. So did John.

"You did this to yourself," John said quietly.

Trevor's eyes darted as distant engines grew louder.

Eli's boat closed the distance.

"They're slowing," Riley said.

"No," Eli muttered. "They're meeting someone."

Another boat appeared through the fog. The two vessels lined up, and one smuggler grabbed a crate.

"They're moving the crates to the other boat!" Riley shouted.

The man lifted the crate...

Blinding searchlights exploded across the water.

"This is the UNITED STATES COAST GUARD! Cut engines and prepare to be boarded!"

Chaos erupted. Smugglers shouted. One tried to run. Another dropped a crate with a thud.

Trevor lunged for Maggie, grabbing her arm. "You're coming with me."

He didn't even see it coming. Maggie twisted sharply, yanking his wrist downward and stepping behind him in one smooth, practiced motion. Her arm slid across his chest and up under his chin, locking his shoulders and pinning his head against her collarbone. She planted her feet wide and leaned back, using her weight to control him.

Trevor's boots skidded on the deck. His face flushed red as he struggled, but Maggie stayed calm, breathing steady, grip firm.

"Grandma?" Alex gasped, eyes wide.

Maggie glanced at him for half a second and gave a tiny smile. "I might be old, but I still have skills."

"FREEZE!" a Coast Guard officer shouted.

Trevor sagged. Maggie released him and stepped back as officers rushed in.

Grandma Maggie turned to the officer. "Took you long enough."

The officer nodded. "Apologies, ma'am. We've been tracking these operations for months. Your involvement helped us close the net."

As dawn painted the sky in hues of pink and orange, Luke, Riley, and Big E reunited with their family on the Coast Guard cutter. Emotions ran high with relief, exhaustion, and a lingering adrenaline buzz. Luke and Alex hugged fiercely. Riley limped over and joined them.

"We thought we lost you," Alex whispered.

Maggie wrapped them all in a tight hug. "Not on my watch."

Dr. Maddox approached the group, her eyes soft with gratitude. "You kids were courageous and tenacious. But promise me, next time, you'll leave it to the professionals."

Luke grinned, teeth still chattering from the cold. "No promises."

Grandma Maggie chuckled, ruffling his wet hair. "That's my boy."

Uncle John placed a hand on Big E's shoulder. "We couldn't have done it without you. Sorry if we misjudged you."

Eli shrugged modestly. " I thought that I had seen light from that old lighthouse, so I had been out poking around the place. Guess some people got the wrong idea about me. Just glad everyone's safe."

Trevor passed in cuffs. Maggie met his eyes. "Looks like the tide finally turned," she said.

He looked away.

As the Coast Guard led the smugglers off, Alex asked, "What happens now?"

"They'll face serious charges," Uncle John said. "Jail. Big fines."

"And the puffins?" Alex asked.

"They're safe," Dr. Maddox said. "Because of you."

Alex smiled.

For a moment, no one spoke. They just watched the sunrise and listened to the waves. They had made a difference. And they knew it.

Chapter 13 – A Job Well Done

A few days after their puffin rescue, the sun climbed high over Seal Island as Captain Emily's boat sliced smoothly through the calm blue water. The salty breeze whipped Luke and Alex's hair as they leaned over the railing, watching the island grow closer with every second.

Neither of them said it out loud, but they both knew this was a moment they would remember forever, especially after everything they had survived.

Out on the water beside them, a research vessel cruised by with Dr. Maddox and her team on board. Below deck, the puffins waited in secure wooden crates, finally on their way home.

"This is amazing," Luke said softly, gripping the railing as Seal Island's rocky cliffs and green slopes came into full view. "It's even more beautiful than I remember."

Captain Emily smiled as she steered. "You boys should be proud. Those birds wouldn't be flying free today if it weren't for you."

Alex shrugged, but he couldn't hide his grin. "Guess a little teamwork goes a long way."

They reached the release site, where Dr. Maddox and several wildlife experts waited near the shore. The crates were lined up carefully, lids unlatched but still closed. Soft rustling came from inside as the puffins shifted, sensing something was about to change.

"Ready?" Dr. Maddox called.

Everyone nodded.

She opened the first crate slowly. For a moment, the puffin just stood there, blinking in the sunlight. Luke held his breath. Then the bird gave a sharp cry, flapped its wings, and launched into the sky.

"It did it!" Alex shouted.

One by one, more puffins followed. Some soared high in the air, others skimming the waves before splashing down. A few floated proudly on the water, while others vanished beneath the surface, already hunting for fish.

"They belong here," Alex said quietly.

"They sure do," Captain Emily agreed. "And thanks to you two, they get a second chance."

Captain Emily clapped them both on the shoulders. "Ever thought about working with wildlife someday? You've got the heart for it."

Luke laughed. "Maybe. But I think we'll stick with mysteries for now."

Alex nodded. "Someone has to solve them."

They all laughed as the boat turned back toward shore. The sun glittered across the waves, and the puffins became tiny dots in the sky, free and safe at last.

Luke glanced at Alex, and they shared a quiet smile. They didn't need to say anything. They both knew what they had been through... and what they had accomplished.

As Seal Island faded into the distance, Luke felt excitement spark inside him.

This mystery was solved.

But he had a feeling their next adventure was already waiting.

Puffins
5 Fun Facts!
1 Puffins are excellent swimmers. They use their wings to "fly" underwater and can dive as deep as 200 feet!
2 They can carry a dozen or more fish in their beaks at once.
3 Puffin couples raise one chick per year and return to the same burrow each spring.
4 Their beaks turn gray in winter and bright orange again in springtime.
5 "Puffin" means "little brother" and scientists call a group of puffins a "circus."